WIDOWMAKER

BIG JOHN MCKENZIE

This book is a work of fiction. All characters, incidents, and dialogue, except for incidental references to public figures, products, or services, are fictional and are not intended to disparage any person, living or dead, or any company or company's products and services.

ISBN 13 978-1-7330743-6-0 (Hardcover)
ISBN 13 978-1-7330743-7-7 (Paperback)

McKenzie, John R.
Widowmaker/ Big John McKenzie

Cover art by Dragan Bilic at Upwork.com

This book is dedicated to my friends, Linda and Sammy.

Thank you for all your support.

CHAPTER ONE

Kansas, 1876

Deputy Marshal Milo Thorne was totin' a gloom. A hard week in the saddle had earned him nothing short of cracked lips, a sun-raw neck, and a sore rump. The only saving grace came into view when he started up a small, reedy knoll along the banks of the muddy Missouri River—Kansas City sprawled out in front of him, three miles due east. A grin dawned on his face, the first in he couldn't remember when. Well over a month had passed since he'd seen the city, yet there she was in all her eminent glory—crowded, smelly, and dull as a spud from the blistering heat.

Milo's grin blossomed full. "Home."

He pulled some mangy jerky from his saddle bag and started gnawing. At the same time, he ran his hand along the muscular neck of his mount. "Yes, sir, Mister Boots, quite the glamorous life we lead." He chuckled at his own lampoon. "We should be able to wrangle a couple of days rest, big fella. We could both use it."

The horse hung its head and picked at the sparse grass.

"Let's get you home. You deserve some proper vittles."

As he raised his reins, a faint dust-trail caught his eye. Horse and rider both tensed, straining to discern the oncoming threat. Milo swung Boots' nose into the wind, edged to the crest of the knoll and narrowed his eyes. "Single rider, coming hard." A larger, secondary dust cloud came into view. "Followed by three or four more."

Milo watched the horsemen; studying their speed, route, and riding formation. His brain ran through the facts at hand, quickly settling on the most logical answer. "Posse."

Milo backed Boots into the patchy reeds, veiling his position, yet affording him sight of the approaching drama. When the single rider was within two-hundred yards, Milo's eyes focused, and an involuntary chuckle escaped his lips.

"The fool's not wearing any clothes. Ol' Nudie's going to have a rump rash."

A second chuckle caught in his throat and his hackles rose.

"Nudie's covered in blood." Milo spurred Boots. "Definitely a fugitive."

Milo reined into a thicket beside the trail, positioned himself in the saddle and waited. Within a minute, pounding hooves announced the approaching rider. Milo steadied Boots and stood in his stirrups. When Nudie galloped abreast wearing nothing but a black derby hat with a hawk feather stuck through its band, Milo pounced, catching his prey in the breadbasket with his shoulder. Both men toppled onto the churned loam and tumbled to a stop. Stunned by the blow, Nudie screamed, then leapt to his feet and ventured to run. Milo tackled him around the knees. The naked man doggedly squirmed himself free and kicked at the lawman's face. Infuriated, Milo clamped his right hand around the man's arm—the sticky, dried blood aiding his grip. Nudie flailed against his captor, becoming a tornado of punches and kicks. Milo held fast, until a wild right cross caught him across the bridge of his nose. He recoiled and the prisoner broke loose. With a burst of energy, Nudie took two steps toward

3

freedom—only to be knocked ass-over-teakettle by a boot heel to the face from the posse's lead rider. Nudie was out cold before his pale behind hit the ground.

Bone-tired and sore from the skirmish, Milo dutifully bound the naked man's hands and stood. All fatigue fell away when he saw the lead rider's face.

Silas Petit, the Marshal of the State of Kansas, shook his head in wonder as he slid to a stop. "You ain't even all the way back in town yet and you've already caused a ruckus?"

Milo grinned at the lanky veteran lawman. "Howdy to you, too."

Roused by the voices, Nudie came to and began struggling against his restraints. "If you two lovebirds are done, I demand you unhand me. This here has nothing to do with the law."

Silas sat tall in his saddle. "Stabbing a woman has everything to do with the law."

"Stabbing a whore ain't illegal," the man shot back.

Silas took off his hat and ran his fingers through his dark hair. "Then why'd you run?"

"I thought you were highwaymen."

"Likely story," Milo replied.

The naked man glared at Milo, taking full-stock of his captor for the first time—including his blunted left wrist. When he spoke, his voice was a hiss. "Set me loose, cripple."

Milo's jaw tightened, as did his grip on the scoundrel's arm. At that moment, Nudie stomped his heel on Milo's toes and spun forcefully. This time the big marshal's grip held true. When Milo regained his wits, he raised his stub to punch the culprit. The calming voice of Senior Deputy Twig Randall brought him back to center. "Don't blame him for your lapse. You're the one you should be mad at."

Milo stiffened, knowing Twig was right. He bit his lip, nodded to the venerable sprite of a lawman, scooped up the naked man, and threw him over the saddle of his horse. Another set of hands began assisting him in binding the prisoner. When they'd finished, the familiar, but out-of-place form of Rod Newby stepped into view.

"What are you doing here, Mute?"

"I came up on an errand for Sheriff Lemure. I was at the Armory when the posse rode out." He gave a grin and shrug. "Figured I'd join the fun."

Newby put the derby back on the naked man's head. Instantly he flailed wildly, kicking Milo's thigh. The big marshal bit back his rage.

"Calm down, Wes," Newby yelled. "You're just digging yourself a deeper grave."

The naked man jerked his head up and spat on the lawman's tin badge.

Calmly, Newby unhasped the star and dried it on his britches, his face showing no emotion. "Fellas," he said. "This here's Wes Harms, from down Loess way—a gentleman of noble breeding."

"Shut up, Mute!" Harms growled. "Or it'll be your job when we get home."

"You ain't going home," Silas barked. "You're under arrest for attempted murder." He turned to his men. "Our work here is done. Let's get back to town."

The posse mounted up for the ride back to Kansas City. Being the most accomplished rider in the group, Twig handled the reins of the mount that carried Wes Harms.

Newby fixed his star on his vest, swung his horse around in the opposite direction and addressed Silas. "I'm halfway home as it is, Marshal. So, if there's no objections, I'll ride south from here."

"Much obliged for the help," Silas replied. "Say howdy to Alf for me."

Newby thumbed his hat and took hold of his reins.

"Mute!" Harms yelled.

"You got something to say, Wes?"

"Get ahold of Galen for me."

"Go to hell, Wes. And when you get there, spit in the Devil's eye, so he can do to you the things my better nature stayed my hand from here today."

"Tell him," Harms scowled, "or I swear, if it's the last thing I do, I'll kill you."

Newby's face hardened. "Tough to do from a prison cell." He reined away and was gone in a flash.

CHAPTER TWO

The ride back to Kansas City was nowhere near as exciting as the ride out. Harms behaved himself, as it's hard to act the fool when tied to the back of a horse with no clothes on. The makeshift peace ended when the posse tied off in front of the Armory—headquarters for the Kansas Marshal's Office. As Milo marched him up the entry steps, Harms sensed imminent danger and upped his tantrum—his voice holding a tint of panic. "I suppose you think you're some kind of tough guy," he chided. "Take these handcuffs off me and let's settle this man-to-man."

The big marshal bit his tongue at the crack. At six feet, six inches in height, Milo knew the taunts to hold only wind.

"You're cowering behind that badge, I can tell," the still-naked man went on. "You wouldn't be so bold if it was just you and me."

Milo stuck the stump of his left arm behind Harms' back and lifted him slightly off the ground to prevent escape. He then used his right hand to open the building's front door.

The scoundrel took another shot at Milo's handicap. "Are you the boss's nephew or something? I can't see them stooping so low as to hire a cripple as a lawman."

As Milo lowered him toward the ground, Harms kicked out his feet, placing one on each side of the door— lunging rearward as he did so. The back of his derby slammed hard against Milo's chin, staggering him. The naked man twisted and nearly broke free, but Milo's massive right hand grabbed a chunk of blond hair and held the lout steady. Harms seized the opportunity to once again spit in Milo's face. The faint remembrance of Twig Randall's placid voice saved the scoundrel from Milo's massive right fist.

Milo forced Harms through the door, past the business counter, and down the corridor toward the decrepit jail. The naked man screamed insults the entire time. The commotion brought busy lawmen out of their offices, half-wondering if a grade school field trip was in the building. Instead they spied a deputy who had been away on a manhunt for over a month, leading a naked madman toward cell number four.

Two steps behind the spectacle, Silas Petit grinned and shook his head. *You don't see wonders like that working in a dry goods store.*

When he'd finished booking his prisoner into custody, Milo ambled down the hall toward his desk: head down, exhausted from his extended trip, and from stifling his temper.

He passed the office of Silas Petit as the boss was hanging his own hat on a nail. "Harms sure tested your mettle; awful impressive that he's still in one piece."

"I kept repeating over and over in my head, *he ain't worth it.*"

"You did well," Silas grinned. "I'm glad you're back. It's hard to convey it over a telegraph wire, but I wanted to tell you face to face that I'm proud of all the work you did in bringing Hal Hampton to justice. He was a bad man."

"Bad men make mistakes," Milo replied to the venerated lawman. "Mistakes make them easy to find. A wise man taught me that."

At that precise moment, Twig Randall entered the room.

"Speaking of the devil," Milo said.

Silas chuckled.

Twig looked between the two men, trying to figure which joke he'd been the butt of. He took in his partner's face. "Your eyes look like two piss-holes in the snow."

"A week straight on a horse does that to a man."

"You haven't been home yet?" Silas asked. "We expected you yesterday."

Milo shook his head. "Boots had a loose shoe, slowed us down."

"Why were you headed into town then?" Twig asked. "We guessed you'd catch some shut-eye before coming back to work."

"I figured it was my duty to check in as soon as I got into Kansas City."

"Consider yourself checked in," Silas added. "Now, get out of my building and go home. You look like you're about to fall over."

"Can't go home now, I've got an arrest report to write."

"I can write the report for you," Twig replied.

"You know you can't do that," Milo said. "The only one who truly saw what happened is me. I caught him; I'll clean him."

Silas nodded. "Life's rough when a man has no integrity, but often it's rougher when he does. Come on Twig, let the man work."

****

Fifty feet away, Wes Harms paced his jail cell like a caged lion, frantically running his fingers along the feather in his hat. Each step he took brought more frustration and corresponding anger. At once, he stopped in his tracks, grabbed the cold steel bars and began to rattle.

The noise drew the attention of the Senior Jailer. The burly man rumbled down the corridor and stopped in front of the unruly noisemaker. "What do you want, Harms?'

"Let me out of here, you miserable fool. I'll have your job for this."

"Sit down and bite your lip. Your bellyaching ain't accomplishing anything."

"I'll do no such thing. I'm an innocent man."

"That's for the district court judge to decide. Now, sit down."

"I can't be guilty. She lived, didn't she?"

"She's lucky she did," the jailer shot back. "By all accounts, the doctor had to sew her up like a Thanksgiving turkey."

"She's a whore!" Harms yelled. "It's not against the law to—"

"She's a human being. That's more'n can be said of you."

Harm's eyes flashed. "You wait until my uncle hears of this! He'll set you straight. He owns the entire town of Loess!"

"He's gonna have to ride up here with a shovel to dig up your carcass if you don't button your lip."

A sneer crossed Harms' mouth. "Are you threatening me?"

"A threat's something that *might* happen," the big jailer flexed his muscles and pointed at the gathering darkness outside the window. "Night's coming and this town'll get noisier than a marching band at a parade, which means no one'll hear you scream. So, one more peep from you and I'll bury you so deep the worms'll need a map to find you."

Harms flinched at the edge in the jailer's voice.

"Button your lip," was the jailer's final warning.

Wes Harms slumped onto the wooden cot that served as his bed and began to weep from anger.

****

Two hours later, Milo had the report written and his office locked up. On his way out, he made a detour and grabbed a month's worth of post from his mailbox. He sauntered out into the dusk, threw the bundle in his saddle bag, and mounted up. His shoulders ached and his bum was saddle-sore.

"Come on, Boots, let's go home." He eyed the bustling street warily. "We ain't stopping, even if the Devil himself's in town."

CHAPTER THREE

Rod Newby eased off the pace as he neared Loess, giving his horse its nose in the gathering darkness, his mind swirling from the excitement of the day. *Nothing like that ever happens in Loess.* His willingness to help in Kansas City filled him with pride—the pride of being on the right side of justice. His hand shifted to his badge without thinking. Suddenly, a vision of the bloody woman in the street came back to him—the cuts and stab wounds and wailing cries still fresh in his memory.

Wes.

Newby shuddered at the name. His false bravado in front of the big city lawmen notwithstanding, Harms' threats cut deep. *My name will be mud in Loess once Reid hears of my part in the matter.* His pride waned. *Maybe the excitement ain't all it's cracked up to be.*

The glint of a campfire caught his eye and piqued his interest. He gently guided his mount through the scrub brush toward the visitor. *I wonder who it is? No one ever comes to Loess. Hopefully it's someone interesting.* His mind conjured images of exotic travelers bringing tales from afar to his sleepy town.

Anything to keep his thoughts off Wes Harms.

****

Andy Steele eased a pot of coffee on the fire and sat back. His thoughts returned to the mission at hand—his cousin: *If I don't find Clancy, Mama's gonna kill me.*

On his ride in, he'd spotted a familiar small town nestled in a dusty valley—Loess, Kansas. "That there's a snake pit," he muttered to himself. *But it's also the last place I saw Clancy.* He shook his head. *That was quite some time ago. He had to have ridden on toward Kansas City by now.*

He threw another log on the fire and spoke to the blossoming flames. "I'll ride into town in the morning and ask around. It's my last hope."

His horse nickered, but he felt no threat so far off the beaten path. Tired of talking to himself, Steele addressed the muscled beast ten feet away in the shadows. "Where'd you go if I turned you free to run, Russ?" The horse shook his head in response, drawing a chuckle from his inquisitor. "Probably to a barn full of hay," Steele laughed, "and in-season mares."

With his eyes focused on the fire and his mind distracted by his horse, Steele did not hear the man approaching in the dark. The rider's call caught him off-guard.

"Hello in the camp!"

Steele scrambled to his holster and drew his weapon. "Who goes there?"

"A friend," came back the answer. "Deputy Rodrick Newby, Loess Sheriff's Office."

Andy Steele relaxed. "Ride in, there's coffee brewing."

The lawman entered the light of the fire with his hands open in front of him.

"Come on in," Steele said. "If you'd have wanted me dead, I'd already be dead. As much attention as I was paying, you could've shot me a hundred times."

Newby laughed. "Just passing through?"

"Well, since you're a man of the law…" Steele proceeded to tell the story of his missing cousin.

Newby listened intently, but couldn't recall seeing Clancy Walker in town. "Sheriff Alf Lemure's the man you want to see. He gets into the office early. Tell him the Mute sent you his way."

"The Mute?"

"That's been my nickname for a long time," Newby smiled. "I keep to myself mostly."

Andy's eyebrows raised. "Nothing to say?"

"No one in Loess is all that interesting to talk to."

The men shared a chuckle.

"Much obliged for the information," Steele said. "Coffee's ready. Can I pour you a cup?"

"I'd love some."

Steele reached for the pot and a hint of color from his arm caught Newby's attention. His dark eyes narrowed and he drew his weapon.

Startled, Andy gasped. "I'll give you the whole pot if you want it!"

"Roll that sleeve all the way up, nice and slow."

Steele did as told.

Newby's eyes widened. He reached into his vest pocket with his free hand, withdrew a yellowed sheet of parchment, and unfolded it. As he glanced at a blotchy mark

18

on Steele's left forearm, a full smile beamed below his over-grown moustache.

"Hal Hampton, you're under arrest for murder." He held the wanted poster aloft and shook it in triumph. "And I'm rich!"

An hour later, Rod Newby noiselessly ushered his prisoner through the front door of the Loess Sheriff's Office, careful not to wake the man behind the corner desk whose hat was pulled down over his eyes. Once he was locked in the single jail cell, Newby cleared his throat.

"Alf."

Sheriff Alf Lemure's eyes shot open, immediately taking in the changes in the room. "Who's that?"

Newby handed his boss the wanted poster. Alf unfolded it, glanced at the prisoner's face, and stood. He crossed to the cell and barked at the prisoner. "Gimme your left arm."

With no particular reason not to, the prisoner obliged.

Alf nodded immediately, turning back to his deputy. "What time is it?"

"Nine-thirty, or thereabouts."

"The judge has already gone home for the day, but it looks like a match. If he escapes, you have the most to lose, so you're on guard duty tonight."

"But Sheriff," the man cried, "that's not me. I'm newly in town, out of Texas!"

"I caught him up on the bluff, casing our town," Newby said.

"I wasn't casing anything," the prisoner replied.

"Then exactly what were you doing?" Alf asked.

"I'm looking for my cousin, Clancy Walker."

Alf's face blanched at the mention of the name. His voice quavered as he spoke. "I'll be back in the morning. We'll take him to the judge first thing."

"So I can get my money?" Newby smiled.

Alf's jaw tightened. "So justice is served."

It was to be a long night on prisoner watch, so Newby set about making a pot of coffee. He was shuffling through desk drawers in search of something edible when the front door opened. Not expecting visitors, he drew his weapon.

The sudden experience of staring down the barrel of a Colt startled Deputy Jeb Thompson. "What the hell, Rod? Put that thing away!"

Newby relaxed, his weapon sliding easily back into its holster. "Sorry, Jeb."

"What are you doing here? It's past the witching hour."

"Counting my money." He picked up the wanted poster for Handsome Hal Hampton and gestured toward the cell.

Thompson's eyes narrowed. "That's him! Does Alf know?"

"He was here when I brought him in."

Thompson whistled between his teeth and sat. "Five-hundred dollars. Well, I'll be…"

"You can be whatever you wanna be," Newby chuckled. "But I'll be the second richest man in town."

"Yeah, well, you've got a long way to go to catch up to Galen Reid, or even Wes Harms for that matter."

Newby's eyes glinted. "Not no more."

"What do you mean by that?"

"Wes is in jail up in Kansas City for attempted murder."

Thompson shot to his feet. "How you say?"

"Stabbed a whore, damned near killed her. I was there when the Kansas Marshals caught him."

Thompson stood stock-still, the wheels of his mind grinding on the information. After a time, he looked Newby in the eye. "Does Reid know?"

"I wasn't planning on telling him."

"The hell you say? If Harms swings and you knew, but didn't tell Reid…" Thompson gave a sneer. "You're as good as dead yourself."

The reality crashed in on Rod Newby and he twitched.

Thompson saw an angle. "How about I go tell Reid, if you're scared to? Wes is a friend of mine. Reid'll appreciate me telling him." *And I'll finally be the golden boy around here.*

Newby read the signs and saw no downside—he'd avoid having to talk to Reid and be off the hook if Wes escaped punishment. He shrugged his shoulders. "Suit yourself."

CHAPTER FOUR

Milo Thorne's spirits rose as he turned down the path that led onto his property. Though past midnight, the full moon illuminated his sturdy house in the ample yard, steadfast and well-built. Through the exhaustion, he smiled. *Damn, I've missed this place.*

Boots seemed to sense the mood change, making way for the barn without hesitation. As they entered the exterior corrals, a pack of wild dogs bolted from the building's wide front door and darted into the shadows of the nearby wheat field. Drained, neither horse nor rider flinched at the canine interruption. Once inside, Milo dismounted and began caring for his travelling companion. He fed, watered, and brushed Boots, then turned him loose in his stall to rest.

The sound of whimpering roused Milo's attention. He lit a lantern and scouted the rushes for the source, finding two small puppies in a bed of straw.

"Somehow I don't think your mama's coming back now that I'm home," Milo sighed. He bent down and rubbed each behind the ears. They rewarded him with licks from their rough tongues. He scooped them up. "Come on, it's more comfortable in the house."

Not knowing what to expect after a month away, Milo entered his house with an abundance of caution. To his surprise, the place was immaculate. He proceeded through the front room into the kitchen, finding the counters clean and the dishes washed and neatly stacked.

"Someone been living here?" he asked the puppies. "You're supposed to keep an eye on the place."

Their confused yips gave him no clues to go on. A note on the gleaming counter caught his eye.

Twig told me you were home. I took
the liberty of sprucing up so you
wouldn't have to. Your linens
are clean, there's fresh milk, and I
restocked the pantry. Welcome back.
I can't wait to see you,
May Randall

Friends like the Randall's are hard to find. A warmth filled Milo's heart. *Friendship built on a solid foundation.* He glanced around the house. *Like this place.* As suddenly as it rose, his mood plunged. *But, I'm alone.* His mind wandered back to a diamond ring laying on a stark marble floor. *Paula.* Without meaning to, he shook his head. "That doors forever closed." As his emotions rose, a weariness radiated from his aching heart outward.

"I could use a hot bath."

Milo put the big kettle on the stove to boil. While he waited, he poured a saucer of milk for the puppies and smiled as they devoured the thick liquid. When the kettle whistled, he filled his tub, stripped off his clothes, and dipped a finger in the water to assure its warmth. As he stepped in, he caught a glimpse of himself in the silver pitcher he'd used to carry hot

25

water—finding his face hard and his eyes sunken. The smooth, raised scar from a bullet-hole on his left shoulder glistened a bright red, contrasting with the whiteness of his skin.

His mind raced. *So, this is what a successful hunt for a murderer looks like?* His own hollow eyes stared back at him. *At what cost?* He thought of Handsome Hal Hampton who was now buried in a trash dump in Colorado. *All the lives lost to a man who cared only for himself.* Once more, he thought of Paula Lowe, the woman who wore his engagement ring for less than a month. *And the love lost.* He shook his head to clear it. *Was it really a success?* The elation of his homecoming waned. The hospitality of May Randall faded from memory, as did the soothing thoughts of his house.

A man's got to feel at home with himself, or no domain will hold his true hearth.

He slumped into the steamy water, allowing the heat to scald his demons.

Once he'd finished his bath, Milo went to the kitchen, finding the puppies wrestling with an old dish towel. He picked through the stack of mail, finding a telegram from Judge Mort Grange of Vermont. His eyes gleamed as he read:

GOOD NEWS FROM HOME. STOP. I FINALLY
SOLD YOUR PROPERTY IN MONTPELIER. STOP.
LARGEST LAND DEAL IN STATE HISTORY.
STOP. CONGRATULATIONS. STOP. EVEN IF
KANSAS IS YOUR RESIDENCE. STOP. YOU ARE
NOW THE RICHEST MAN IN VERMONT. STOP.
DETAILS TO FOLLOW. STOP. MORT.

Milo said a silent thank you to his father, then scooped up the puppies and went to his bedroom. He placed the puppies on the bed, next to a copy of Marcus Aurelius' *Meditations*. When he settled in, the fur-balls each chose a side and curled up in the soft sheets. Milo pondered his feelings, contrasting the comfort afforded by his father's lucrative will against the simpler pleasures of a good book, fresh linens, and playful puppies.

"Ahh, the age-old argument," he muttered to the sleepy pair. "External security versus internal satisfaction."

No use choosing sides, he thought. *I like both options.*

He nodded without thinking. "You're going to be just fine."

Am I talking to them, or myself?

Milo smiled and opened his book.

27

CHAPTER FIVE

"There are men who cloak themselves in the Devil's vestments from the first decision they make as a young'un…" Judge Sturgis Rathbone paused and glared at the shackled man who stood before him. The judge ran his right hand across the stubbled chin of his bulldog face, wetted his lips, bent slightly at the waist, and spat a long, viscous chaw of tobacco into the spittoon by his right foot. He wiped his chin with his sleeve and looked back at the harrowed prisoner. "And by all accounts, you're such a beast. You got anything to say before I pass judgment?"

The prisoner gave a furtive glance at the tall, angular man who had a firm grip on his left elbow. Sheriff Alf

Lemure's head gave an almost imperceptible nod, freeing the prisoner to speak.

The shackled man swallowed and turned back to the judge. "Sir, I didn't do it. I'm not the man you think I am. My name is Andy Steele. I've never heard of Hal Hampton. I was in town looking for my cousin. I'm innocent. I swear to you!"

The declaration did not produce the desired result. In fact, the opposite effect was set in motion. The judge's eyes narrowed and his face flushed. "Mister Hampton, this is not the first time I have heard you say that, but it will definitely be the last." He opened the leather valise on his desk, withdrew a single yellowed parchment, unfolded it, and held it up for the prisoner to see. The shackled man blanched. A face drawn in charcoal stared back at him as if he'd gazed into a polished mirror.

WANTED FOR MURDER
HAL HAMPTON AKA HANDSOME HAL
FIVE FEET AND TEN INCHES TALL, 170 POUNDS
THREE-INCH BIRTHMARK ON LEFT FOREARM
USE CAUTION, HEAVY TRIGGER FINGER
REWARD $500, DEAD OR ALIVE

The judge dropped the wanted poster onto the desk and sat back in his chair. "Lift his left sleeve, Alf."

The sheriff grabbed the cuff of the prisoner's shirtsleeve and yanked so hard that the button popped off and fell to the floor. About two fingers above the wrist, a wine-color birthmark came into view. Judge Rathbone sneered as the blotchy flesh became evident.

"It's just a splash," the prisoner plead. "Not three inches!"

"Close enough for me," the judge growled. "Hal Hampton, as the keeper of the public peace for Anderson County, in the great state of Kansas, I hereby sentence you to death by hanging for the crimes you've committed."

The prisoner jerked hard against his chains. "No! I'm Andy Steele. I'm innocent!"

"Enough!" the judge barked. "Take him to Devil's Nob and swing him from the Widowmaker."

Once more, the shackled man shrieked. "I'm not Hampton. I'm innocent!"

"Mister Hampton, it takes about ten minutes to ride out to the Nob," Rathbone said, his voice void of empathy. "Therefore, in about ten minutes and thirty seconds you can argue your case with the Almighty himself. Get him out of my sight, Alf!"

Sheriff Lemure clamped down on the prisoner's arm and yanked him hard toward the door. The condemned man's legs buckled and he lurched forward, landing on his knees. He began to sob. "I'm innocent. It wasn't me."

Lemure pulled him roughly to his feet and marched him out the door onto the sun-drenched street.

Judge Rathbone waited until the man's cries died in the distance, then opened the top-drawer of his desk and pulled out a bottle of whiskey and a pair of shot glasses. With a practiced hand, he yanked out the cork and poured two drinks. He sat the bottle on the desktop and silently slid one jigger to his right. The stubby, rheumatic fingers of Galen Reid wrapped themselves around the glass and drew it toward his round face.

"Well, I must say, that was unpleasant." Reid's strong Texas drawl belied his weak presence. He threw back his head and took the full glass of whiskey in one shot.

Judge Rathbone blinked hard when he noticed Reid's creped jowls jiggling under his wobbly chin. He laughed inwardly. Knowing that Reid was a Boston transplant made his well-practiced accent even more humorous. *He's false from his piggy-feet to his sweaty brow*. The judge slammed back his own drink and drew a hot breath through his teeth. "The loss of dignity in a begging man is always unpleasant— and murderers *always* beg."

Reid shifted in his seat and faced the judge. "I have no interest in the whimpering of a madman, Sturgis. I'm here to collect on a favor owed." Reid wrapped his liver-spotted right hand around his pearl-handled cane, pointing it at the Judge. "You know what I have asked, and you know what my reaction will be if you fail to agree. What is your answer?"

To the casual observer, Judge Rathbone gave no outward reaction. Perhaps those who knew him best would have noticed the tell-tale signs of discomfort that the question brought forth: tensed facial muscles, flared nostrils, and a tic of his left eyelid. That said, no one could detect the inner discomfort he felt in acquiescing to the despicable human toad that sat before him.

Reid leaned forward, anticipating the Judge's response.

Even in deep contemplation of the ethical trap he set upon himself, Rathbone could not help but hear the chair screaming for relief from Reid's enormous bulk.

Reid smacked his lips impatiently. "May I remind you, Sturgis, a debt is a debt, no matter one's lofty standing in *local government*."

Judge Rathbone felt pressure welling in his sinuses. "Don't push me, Galen. I am not a man to be trifled with."

Reid rolled his eyes. "Nor am I, Sturgis. Your entire life revolves around your *honorable status*." Reid grumbled the last two words in as sarcastic a manner as he could muster. "And I can bring your so-called *honor* to its knees in the blink of an eye."

The judge drew a steadying breath and his shoulders slacked in defeat. "This will conclude our dealings, Galen. I want your word on that."

"I swear it on Clancy Walker's cross."

Judge Rathbone flinched at the name hurled at him like a dart. "Then consider it done."

"When?"

"By tomorrow night."

Reid grunted and pushed himself from the chair. He struggled to his feet and straightened his rumpled jacket. "Tonight."

"I couldn't possibly…"

Reid cut across the Judge's words. "Yes, you *can.* Make it happen."

"How do you know this is even true? I've received no telegraphs."

Reid's jowls tightened. "It seems as though one of our local badge-carriers was there when they illegally arrested my nephew." Reid straightened his lapels. "And yet the coward lacked the backbone to tell me himself. Luckily, Jeb Thompson was compassionate enough to let me know." Reid's face went stern. "By all accounts, Sturgis, it's true, and I want Wes back unharmed."

Judge Rathbone slumped in his chair as if crushed by his own conscience. Reid took a step forward and placed his porcine hand on the seated man's shoulder. "Do not despair, my dear Sturgis. You're a powerful man around here. Why, you are quite possibly the second most powerful man in this county."

Sturgis Rathbone shrugged off the unwanted gesture.

Galen Reid smiled with disdain and toddled to the door. As he pushed it open, he turned. "Little do I need to remind you, Sturgis—do not lose sight of who is number one."

CHAPTER SIX

Loess, Kansas was typical of most mid-West frontier towns. Torrential rains followed by intense, baking sun had hard-fired the ground into a powdery silt. Wagons, horses, and cattle passing through whirled up the pasty-white dust, distributing it everywhere on the plank-board buildings that constituted the hardscrabble town. A dry-goods store, two saloons, a one-room barber shop that doubled as the undertaker's office, a two-story hotel that also housed a squalid bordello, and the tiny office of the court and assay office were all it held.

Sheriff Lemure marched his prisoner through the thick dust covering Main Street. The sweltering heat had driven the residents inside, but dozens of eyeballs peered through windows to see who was making all the ruckus outside. Alf stopped in front of the modest building that served as both the Sheriff's office and jail. "Shanks, Thompson, get out here."

Two men stepped through the door, eying the shackled man with interest. The older of the pair was gangly; a salt-and-pepper beard covered most of his raw-boned face. The other was tall and thick, with veiled blue eyes and a mane of dirty blond hair.

Alf snapped at them. "Mount up, we're riding out to the Nob."

Shanks Morris grinned and scuttled toward the stables like a water skeeter, his left leg locked at the knee by an old war injury.

Jeb Thompson tugged at the rope that held up his britches, spat into the dust, and stared at Alf. "You need both of us to go? It's just one greenhorn. Where's the Mute? Why ain't he riding out?"

Alf pierced Thompson with a stare. "He's a murderer, not a greenhorn. I gave the Mute the morning off on account he spent the night in the jail with the prisoner."

"He don't want to watch him swing?"

"He's seen plenty of men swing. This here ain't no different. I said mount up. You disobeying an order?"

The big deputy spat and swept a greasy lock of hair from his face. "Nah, let me get my hog-leg. I just got back from the bawdy house, so my horse is already tacked."

"Move your hips then. I want to get shut of this business before dinner."

Alf wrapped one of his sinewy arms around the prisoner's waist and hoisted him onto a strawberry roan tethered to the hitching post. He pulled a short length of rope from his saddle and tied the prisoner's feet together under the belly of the steed.

"Make a run for it, Hampton, and you'll slide off. If that happens, he'll drag you till I tell him to stop running."

"My name's not Hampton. You've got the wrong man! I've got no reason to run!"

Thompson stepped onto the street, buckling his gunbelt. "Who'd he murder, Sheriff?"

"Dunno. The warrant's out of Kansas City."

The prisoner shifted. "I've never been to Kansas City. Can't you just take me there so the witnesses can tell you I'm not the killer? Please, Sheriff!"

"It's a full-day ride to Kansas City. After two hours I'd probably shoot you for whining. Now, shut your flap. I got no

37

patience for your yammering. You heard the Judge's decision and so did I."

Thompson mounted up and Alf handed him the reins to the prisoner's horse. "I'll ride point and Shanks can take up the rear. Keep your eyes and ears open."

"You think someone will try to spring him?"

Alf's eyes narrowed. "You ever been appointed to anything other than your deputy job?"

A puzzled look crossed Thompson's face. "No, why?"

"Well, I seem to recall my being appointed Sheriff of this County. That means I give the orders around here. Is that too hard for you to remember?"

"No."

"Good, because I'm getting tired of you chewing my fat all day long. Swallow your tongue before I cut it out of your head."

Thompson spat on the street; his jaw tight. "Sure."

Shanks led his horse out of the stables and climbed into the saddle.

"Ride drag. Keep your head on a swivel," Alf barked at him.

"Yes, sir, Sheriff."

Alf turned in his saddle and faced his insolent deputy. "Now, that's how you answer your boss." He reined his horse hard and took off at a gallop.

As they crossed in front of the ramshackle courtroom, Sturgis Rathbone's stepped onto the street. "Alf!"

The Sheriff's head snapped in the direction of the voice. His trained eye caught the immense bulk of Galen Reid waddling from the Judge's office and out onto the street. He made a mental note of the dandy's finery and how out of place he was on the open frontier. *I wonder what he's up to? Nothing good, I'm sure.*

Rathbone's bark snapped the Sheriff from the thought. "Don't dawdle. Swing him quick and get your hide back here. I've got something I need you and the boys to do for me."

Alf nodded and turned his eyes toward their destination. *So much for dinner.*

On a patchy knoll outside town, sat a solitary, gnarled bur oak tree. The grizzled giant might have reigned over that hill for a thousand years, but it had only existed in Alf's world for the last five. It was the first thing he'd seen of the town as he rode north from Amarillo and it was the last thing twenty-nine of his prisoners had seen since he'd been appointed Sheriff. Its single, godforsaken limb had known men ranging from the meek to the infamous. He spared little thought about where his current charge fit into that spectrum.

One more for the buzzards was his only glancing thought.

The ride through town and up the gentle slope to Devil's Nob was excruciating for the lawmen. The condemned prisoner alternated between unabashed crying to full-throated shrieks. Tired of the prisoner's antics, Alf lengthened the distance between himself and his deputies. As a result, he was the first to ride into the clearing surrounding the twisted giant and its notorious weather-worn branch.

Widowmaker.

He pulled his bandana over his nose to break the stench from the decaying flesh of the three men who had already met their deaths on the storied arm of the ancient tree. His eyes darted from one to the next, his mind recalling the crimes that brought them to their ends.

Closest to the trunk, Hippo James…rape. We had to hang him closest to the trunk so the fat bastard wouldn't take the whole shebang down when the horse ran out from under him.

In the middle, Ty Brakeman…horse thief. Ugliest man in Kansas and a swindler at that. Good riddance.

On the end, Vern Ashford. Shot a man in a card game. He probably shouldn't have swung, but when Sturgis says he swings, he swings.

Alf stole another glance at the limb and sighed. *Three men in less than two weeks and another to follow.* He rubbed the back of his neck and surveyed the crowded branch. *A man's gotta do his job.*

After making a mental note of where he wanted to place the noose for Hampton, Alf rode a quick circle to chase away two opportunistic buzzards. When he'd finished, he reined his horse at the edge of the clearing to wait for his deputies. The dust-covered expanse of Loess spread out below him. *Growing like a weed. The land provides the water and soil, and Galen Reid produces the fertilizer.*

Thompson topped the knoll and led the prisoner to the base of Widowmaker. Alf whistled and Shanks spurred his horse to a trot. Within seconds, the hanging party was in place.

Shanks looked up at the distressed limb that bore the weight of three men. "You want I should cut those fellas down, Sheriff?"

"Nope, leave 'em as a reminder to visitors that we take the law serious in Loess. Once the buzzards pick this one clean, we'll come up and care for the carcasses."

The prisoner burst into tears. "Please, Sheriff...please!"

"Get on with it, Jeb."

The big deputy reached into his saddle bag and drew out a morral that held a freshly tied noose. Alf pointed to a spot and Thompson threw the long end of the rope around the limb. He tied it off, then placed the noose around the crying man's neck. The prisoner winced as the burlap bag was lowered over his head. Thompson placed a long, rusty key in the shackles and removed them, then tied the man's hands loosely behind his back with a thin rope. The prisoner's horse twitched to run, but Alf held it by the reins.

When Thompson finished, Alf spoke. "You got anything you want to say?"

The prisoner's speech was full of terror, but clear. "I didn't do anything wrong!"

Shanks laughed out loud. "Famous last words of a dead man."

Alf held out his hand to quiet his deputy. "Hal Hampton, by order of the honorable Judge Sturgis Rathbone,

42

you are to be hanged by your neck until you die. As the head executioner of this county, I will now carry out those orders."

The prisoner took a deep breath and Alf saw the burlap drawn into his mouth by the force of the air. The prisoner straightened. "Hold on, I *do* have something to say..."

The three lawmen went silent, sensing the newfound rage in the condemned man's voice.

The prisoner heeled his mount in the ribs. "I'll see you all in Hell!"

The horse jumped and the noose snapped taut, ripping the murderer from its back. The rope bit into the condemned man's neck like a rattlesnake. The last thing he heard was the three men laughing and jeering at his wildly swinging body.

Alf didn't wait for the corpse to settle before barking the order to leave. As they passed the twitching body of the murderer, Shanks instinctively kicked out at the man's swaying legs.

"You're the only one bound for hell today."

"Let's ride," Alf snapped, "the Judge has work for us."

The three-man hanging-party spurred their horses over the crest of Devil's Nob and were four-hundred yards away before the doomed man drew his last breath.

****

The prisoner felt shadows of unconsciousness crawling across his brain like an unwanted guest. Only his inner-conviction helped him fight it off.

I'm innocent.

He kicked hard, his feet searching for the horse he knew was no longer there.

I'm not Hal Hampton.

He kicked again—his last, dying act.

Propelled by the final burst of effort, he swung slowly, the weight of his body tightening the noose.

His world faded to black.

If not for the darkness, the prisoner's hopes would have surely soared at the resounding snap of the fracturing limb. If not for the distance gained by their furious riding, the hanging party would have surely witnessed the failure of the hoary branch— and heard the muffled thump of Andy Steele's body hitting the soft, dusty earth below the now limbless Widowmaker.

CHAPTER SEVEN

As the three lawmen entered the dusty town, Alf yelled, "You two head back to the office. Water your horses and be ready for action. I'll go see Sturgis and find out what he has in store for us." The deputies nodded and sped down Main Street. Alf reined up in front of the tiny courthouse and tied off his horse. He took off his hat and swatted his clothes to shake off the heavy covering of grime. Once satisfied, he rapped on the door and heard Sturgis beckon him inside.

The Judge sat in his chair, tapping his fingers to silent music. "How'd it go?"

Alf hung his hat on a hook and stood facing the weary countenance of the man behind the desk. "It was an easy one.

The blame fool heeled his own horse and hung himself. He was still flailing when we rode out."

"How do you know he's dead?"

"You condemn 'em, Sturgis, I swing 'em. I've done it right twenty-nine times before. Take my word for it, this one isn't climbing down alive."

The judge nodded, but his eyes would not make contact with the sheriff. Alf read the body language like a fresh track in the snow. "I sense some bad news headed my way. Hit me with both barrels. I ain't suited to no subtlety."

When the Judge took a deep breath, Lemure knew his hunch was right.

"I got some unpleasant business for you to send the boys on."

"Go on, I'm listening."

"I need them to ride up to Kansas City." Sturgis shifted in his chair. "The marshals have Wes Harms in jail. I need them to vouch for his alibi on my account and bring him back."

"Can you honestly alibi for him?"

Sturgis dropped his eyes and didn't answer.

"Dammit, Sturgis. We can't do that!"

The judge's eyes raised slowly. "Does the name Clancy Walker mean anything to you?"

"So be it," Alf growled through clenched teeth. "I'll go myself. I'm not putting my men in a predicament on Reid's account. I'll leave Shanks in charge and cut out in the morning."

"I thought that might bring you around, but I need you to go now. Harms is in a spot of trouble and the constable might not wait till you get there."

"A hanging offense?"

Sturgis shrugged. "Reid doesn't know for sure, but let's just assume he isn't being held for loitering."

Alf bit back his rage at the predicament.

The Judge noted the Sheriff's balled fists. "You got something to say? Spit it out."

"I'm already weary of Reid bullying the both of us with that name."

The judge's shoulders slumped. "Me too, Alf. I made it perfectly clear that this was the end of it. I made him give his word."

"Reid's word has as much weight as an acorn in a tornado," Alf replied through pursed lips.

"Are you done airing your lungs?"

Alf tilted his head.

Sturgis ran his fingers through his scruffy, snow-colored hair, and his voice softened. "He's got us corralled, Alf. Neither one of us can answer to his claims." The Judge slid two official-looking documents toward the Sheriff. "You'll need these in Kansas City."

Alf snapped up the documents at the same time Sturgis slid the Hal Hampton wanted poster across the desk. "While you're up there, you might as well collect the reward money for the last one on the limb. The Mute's got a rightful claim to it."

With hands palsied from rage, Alf folded it and slipped it inside his duster. Without a word, he nodded to leave.

The judge stood, leaned forward, and gripped the edges of his desk. "Alfred, my old friend, never lose sight of the fact that, while it might not weigh much, an acorn in a tornado can kill both of us just as dead as any .44 slug."

CHAPTER EIGHT

It was the smell that brought Andy Steele around—the thick
rank musk of death—but it was the heat that forced his full
consciousness. Newly limbless, Widowmaker offered little
shade. The scorching sun broiled the nape of his neck and
baked the surrounding horror into a scene from a fetid charnel
house. With an enormous effort, Steele freed his hands from
the loose ropes that bound them, and ripped off the burlap
sack with his right hand. He immediately retched. Steele sat
up quickly, too quickly, and nearly passed out. He looked
down at his hands and saw them covered in a rust-colored
layer of—his mind raced for identification of this foreign—
scum. He sat up, glanced around, blacked out, and didn't wake
again until nightfall.

The succeeding survey of his surroundings went little better. A combination of waning sunlight and a full moon provided adequate light to reveal the ghastly scene around him. The remains of three decaying bodies were outlined in the soft dirt; the outward pattern of internal liquids made it clear they'd burst upon hitting the ground. To make matters worse, the remaining fluids had exploded outward when the massive limb of the ancient oak fell onto the pudding-like bodies of the three doomed men. Steele closed his eyes. *I'm covered in human residue.* His stomach lurched and vomit joined the entrails on his shirt. *But you're alive and can move about.* He gathered himself and cast about to assess his situation. His breath caught at the carnage. *If I was hanging with them, how did the branch miss me?* He searched his memory. *I was swinging.* He pushed himself to his feet and the meager lights of Loess came into view. *In the morning they'll see the tree and come for me.*

Without a plan or a chance, Andy Steele bolted for freedom.

CHAPTER NINE

Wasting no time, Alf Lemure snagged his posse roll and saddled a fresh horse. Shanks Morris and Jeb Thompson came out onto the raised boardwalk to see their boss off.

"You're in charge while I'm gone, Shanks. Don't do anything I wouldn't do."

Thompson's face reddened. "Why's he in charge? I'm senior to him."

"Because, I don't trust you."

The words hit harder than any fist.

Shanks Morris fought back a grin as Thompson retreated to the office in a fury.

As Alf mounted up, Rod Newby arrived for his workday. "Going somewhere?"

"Riding up to Kansas City on the Judge's orders."

"Want some company? I could collect my reward money."

Alf nodded and slapped his reins. "Let's giddy-up."

The ride north was slow on account of a late-afternoon rain. Reaching the point of exhaustion at around the three-quarter mark, they made camp for the night in a shallow, rocky draw. Still tired from the night prior, Newby was asleep almost before his boss was out of the saddle.

After he'd fed and watered his horse, Alf cleared a spot beyond the fire's direct light and untied his posse roll. Five years on the job had prepared him for instant action and the bundle was a testimony to that experience. The roll consisted of a thick horse blanket, a coarse wool blanket, and a ration of dried beef strips. *Everything a man on the run needs to survive.* He threw the horse blanket on the ground, laid down, pulled the wool blanket over him and closed his eyes.

Well, this ain't gonna work. He reached under the horse blanket, dislodged a sharp-edged rock, flipped it into the darkness, then laid back down and stared up at the crystal-clear sky.

Clancy Walker's face wandered smack-dab into the middle of his thoughts.

Alf's mind grasped at the few details he could remember of the fateful night. Galen Reid, Wes Harms, Sturgis, and a fresh-faced stranger, Clancy Walker, had joined him for a high-stakes poker game at Reid's house. The whiskey flowed freely, and both he and Sturgis drank far more than their livers had the capacity to filter. Walker started winning big, eventually wiping out the savings of the lawman and the magistrate. His senses numbed by drink; Sturgis passed out on Reid's gilded couch. When his money dried up, Alf excused himself from the game. That was all he remembered until morning when he found himself on the chintz sofa next to the judge. Upon waking, Alf heard raised voices through the pounding in his head—Reid and Harms arguing over some sort of "accident." He remembered rousing Sturgis and the two of them sitting up at the same time—only to see the body of Clancy Walker dead in a pool of his own blood.

The cobwebs inside Alf's brain were thick and impenetrable, but he recalled Sturgis reacting first. "What the hell happened?"

As if reading a script, Reid had answered, "You don't remember?"

Sturgis had shaken his head and muttered a simple, "No."

Reid had smiled and held out his arm to Harms as if warning him to silence. He pointed at the body. "You accused this—boy—of cheating, Sturgis. He got the drop on both of you. Alf there ended the discussion with his Peacekeeper. Rudely, both of you up and passed out, leaving me with a dead body in my front room."

Alf recalled the confusion of the moment, the faint memory of thumbing back the hammer of his weapon, and the horror of finding a spent cartridge in the chamber.

The shrill hoot of a lonesome owl brought Alf back to the present. It had only been a week since the ill-fated poker game, and not a precious second passed where he hadn't washed and re-washed his brain for insights on the incident— finding only the faintest hints of traction in the whiskey-mired memory. Laying there on his earthbound bedroll, he shook his head. *That was a bad night brought on by bad decisions.*

****

Back in Loess, Sturgis sat alone nursing a whiskey in the nearly empty Irishman Saloon, his mood as dull as his senses. His face reddened as Galen Reid pulled up a chair and sat.

Not bothering with niceties, the fat man simply grunted, "Well?"

The judge swallowed his own bile. "Alf rode out a few hours ago."

Reid's jowls formed a half-smile.

The Judge drained his glass. Unable to contain himself, a barb of sarcasm slipped past his lips. "What's Harms hold over you, Galen?"

Three whiskeys into his own evening, Reid's normally solid external walls crumbled. He surprised Sturgis with an answer. "He's my sister's boy. She died of the grippe when he was a youngster. Her final wish was that I raise him as my own."

Sturgis felt something forming in his heart along the lines of empathy for Reid—until the fat man's dialogue continued.

"He's a good boy," Reid said. "Worthy of your respect. The fact that I might have spoiled him to the point of damage is beyond your business."

"For a young man coddled within the arms of luxury, he holds a bitter hatred for the world."

"Wouldn't you if your mama died and left you as a child?" Reid shifted in his chair, as well as his approach.

"Why Wes is who he is, will no longer be a topic for us to bandy about. I've raised him in the best way I know. When I see him, I see a boy that my sister would be proud of. Therefore, I'm proud of him—and who he is."

"You can cast all the light you wish," Sturgis growled. "But his heart walks on the dark side of the street. He's a demon."

"That's a possibility," Reid smirked as he stood. "But he's my demon, so you'll treat him as such."

"You can both go to hell on my account."

Galen Reid offered an empty chuckle. "The first people we'd meet when we arrived would be you and that no-account Sheriff you call a friend." Reid leaned in. "Being rich and powerful is not a crime, Sturgis, but murder is. In that vein, you can both go to hell on Clancy Walker's account."

The judge bit his tongue at the dead man's name.

Reid straightened his jacket and readied to leave. "You're not required to like me, *Your Honor*, but you are beholden to my wishes. I'd suggest you heed them."

As Reid disappeared behind the bar, the Judge's anger welled. He drank straight from the bottle for the remainder of the evening.

CHAPTER TEN

Change is a constant. Some men fight it, in the way they fight death—but it is inevitable. For some, change is gradual, as unnoticed as a single gray hair in a dark beard. For Andy Steele, change came like a flash of lightning; from innocent wanderer to wanted murderer in the instant of a false accusation. The change haunted his dreams.

Andy woke with a start. The cool, dusty straw that covered him had caked into the available fluids of his body, drying out his mouth and crusting over his nose. His neck burned where the noose had bit in, and his body ached as a result of his fall from Widowmaker's failed branch. He sat up and rubbed his parched mouth.

Water or death.

With the light of the moon illuminating his path, he got to his knees and moved quietly through stacked hay bales of the barn until he reached the lone window in his hideaway. Moving slowly to avoid detection, Andy crept to the sill and peeked out at his surroundings. Below him lay a sprawling single-story home, lit from the inside by bright gas lamps. His eyes scoured the area for the one object he desired—the water trough. He recoiled when he heard a door open on the side of the house, but took a chance and glimpsed out the window. The soft interior light of the house backlit the outline of a heavy man carrying a bucket. Andy's eyes followed the man intently until he heard the one sound he desired most—the dipping of a bucket into water.

It's right below me.

He waited until the man's footsteps retreated, before once again peering out the window. The moment the door to the house closed, the moon returned as the sole source of light. Andy moved quickly to the ladder and slid down to the floor of the barn. The door to the yard was well-used and opened silently. He dropped to his belly and low-crawled to the base of the trough. Fighting against his own thirst, Andy raised himself slowly to his knees, cupped his hands, and quietly dipped them into the cool liquid. The first trickle crossing his lips overwhelmed his senses and he was soon frantically splashing his hands in the water in an attempt to sate his thirst. The door to the house yawned opened, filling the yard with an opaque light. Andy flattened himself against the trough.

"Who's out there?" yelled a shrill voice.

He held his breath, poised to run if detected.

The heavy footsteps of the resident stopped at the edge of the raised wooden deck. Andy used the light to check his surroundings, spying a heavily-laden apple tree nearby.

"Damned animals," the heavy man grumbled.

The footsteps retreated into the house and the door closed, once again plunging the yard into darkness. Andy took one last handful of water, hastily picked three apples and scrambled into the barn. Once nestled back in the loft, he munched on the fruit and pondered his situation.

No one's tracked me here, so I'm safe. There's water—he took a bite of apple—*and food. It's best if I lay low here and let things settle.*

He finished chewing and laid his head in the dry straw. *After that, who knows?*

CHAPTER ELEVEN

Dawn broke, crisp and clear on the trail. Alf Lemure hastily drank a cup of coffee as he packed his kit. The Mute was already up and champing at the bit to go. Alf whistled for his horse, hearing it rustling through the underbrush within seconds. The buckskin received two carrots and a stale biscuit for his loyalty while the Sheriff devoured his trail breakfast of warm coffee and beef jerky.

"Come on, Alf, let's get a move on," the Mute exclaimed, "I've got a reward waiting."

At half-past noon, they crested a small hill and the skyline of Kansas City unfolded before them. They reined up to let catch their breath and take in the burgeoning city.

"What a monstrosity," Alf whistled. "There'll be a hundred thousand people living there before long. Big city, small brains." The density of humans and their accompanying complicated lives made the small-town sheriff uncomfortable.

"Ah, it's not so bad." Newby replied. "The folks I met seemed genuine. Plus, that's where my money is."

They paused only long enough for the thought to register, before spurring their mounts toward the maze of buildings, corrals and homes that made up the bustling cattle town. Never a foot-dragger, Alf rode straight toward The Armory.

"Let's get your money first. There'll be no time to stop with Harms in tow."

"Yep, I don't want the contemptible bastard to know I'm carrying that kind of cash," Newby chuckled. "So, I'd rather have it stowed away before we head back."

They ambled up the steps and pushed through the unlocked door. At the front desk sat a mouse of a lady—thin body, thin hair, and a thin voice.

"Can I help you?"

Alf pulled the wanted poster out of his vest and unfolded it, sitting it on the desk. "We're here to collect the reward on this scoundrel."

"Your name?"

"Alfred Lemure, Sheriff of Anderson County."

The woman scratched the information in a ledger and looked up. "Obviously you did not bring him in alive. Do you have proof of death?"

Alf produced a second sheet of paper. "I have a sworn affidavit from the Honorable Sturgis Rathbone declaring the death of Hal Hampton." He handed it over.

"I see. Give me one minute."

The woman slid off her chair, trudged across the room and through an interior door. Alf spun his hat in his hands as he waited, while Newby fidgeted in anticipation. After a short period, the door opened and a man-mountain stepped through. The Sheriff recognized him instantly. At least six-feet, six-inches tall, and dressed in a black broadcloth suit, the brute was the manifestation of a scowling human-bear mix.

A crooked smile jumped onto the big man's mouth. "Howdy, fellas. It's been quite a piece…"

"Howdy, Milo," Alf replied. "I think the last time I saw you was about six months ago."

"Might have been. What brings you two up to the big city?"

"I'm here to collect the reward on Handsome Hal Hampton," Newby said. "I captured him outside Loess. We hung him yesterday."

The giant held out Alf's parchment. "Well, this is the official wanted poster, but I have to tell you, you're going have a hell of a time collecting any reward on Hampton."

Newby's eyes narrowed. "Why's that?'

"I killed him last month. The fella you hung must've been a ghost."

The Loess lawmen shared a wide-eyed glance, then turned back to Milo.

"I tracked Hampton all the way to Colorado," Milo went on. "The fool tried to kill me, but Mr. Peacemaker foiled his plans." He studied the pained look on the sheriff's face. "Did you hang the wrong fella, Alf?"

Lemure pointed to his left forearm. "He had a mark. We went on that and his looks."

"Was it a full three inches like the poster said?"

Alf's mouth opened and closed several times, but only one word escaped. "He…"

The big man took a step forward. "Alf?"

Startled, Lemure looked up.

"Snap out of it, man. Answer my question," Milo barked.

The fog lifted and Alf gathered himself. "Yeah, yeah, we did. The picture was exact and he had a damn birthmark on his left forearm."

Milo leaned in. "But was it a full three inches like the poster said?"

"Well, maybe it was more like one inch, but there was a damned mark."

"Three full inches." Milo jabbed his stump at the parchment. "The Hampton I killed had three full inches!"

Alf blanched and his shoulders slumped.

"That's sloppy work, Alf. You're a better lawman than that." Milo rubbed the back of his neck. "I'd assume Sturgis ordered the hanging. Didn't he follow due diligence before passing sentence?"

Alf nodded. "He saw the mark, same as I did." His eyes came up to the marshal. "Everything else was a dead-on match, Milo."

Milo nodded slowly. "None of us are perfect, but you know I'll have to look into it."

Lemure's nostrils flared and his eyes bore into the big man.

The Marshal took note. "Curb your anger, Alf. I'll ride back with you and check things out. Maybe look over the body if it's still intact. When I'm done poking about, I'll buy you all a steak at the Irishman and we can kick around old times."

Alf's shoulders relaxed. "I'm sorry, Milo. It's just that there couldn't have been a more exact ringer." He let out a long, whistling breath. "That poor clod that we strung up. He screamed and cried all the way to the end of the noose. Maybe I should have been all ears."

"You got other business up here?" Milo asked. "It doesn't figure that the Sheriff himself would ride this far to collect on a reward. That's what deputies are for."

"Nah, we've got other business," Alf answered.

"Even less pleasurable than missing out on five-hundred dollars," Newby added.

Milo's eyes widened. "It doesn't pertain to that Wes Harms character from down your way does it?"

Alf's face reddened. "Yeah, why do you ask?"

The Marshal stood to his full height. "That one is a golem of fecal matter. Hopefully you're here to watch him swing."

Neither of the Loess lawmen answered.

65

"What the hell, Alf. You're here for his benefit?"

The Sheriff cleared his throat, as he did not want to say what was about to spill out of his mouth. "Yes, sir. Sturgis sent me with a sworn testimony to his alibi."

"Judge Rathbone's word is good with me, but this smells of a rat." Milo shook his head in disgust. "I'll ride back with you, simply to assure Harms is gone. That said, this development doesn't make me happy."

Alf's eyes fixed on his own feet. "Me either."

Milo bent at the waist until his mouth was near the Sheriff's ear. His voice was low, but stern. "You're a good man, Alf. One of the best. I don't know what you and Sturgis have stepped into, but make sure you scrape it off your boots. I hope you two are on the square. Friends or not, I'll do my sworn duty. Come on back to my office whilst I chase your skunk out of my jail."

CHAPTER TWELVE

Milo Thorne paced back-and-forth across Silas Petit's office as he laid out the situation of the possible hanging of an already dead man in Loess. Silas and Twig listened intently, while the Loess lawmen sat with their eyes hooded.

When Milo finished, he sat on the corner of the desk. "Sound about right, Alf?"

"Every word of it," the sheriff replied.

Silas rubbed his temple. "Even if it's a case of mistaken identity, we'll have to do a thorough investigation. You agree to that, Alf?"

"Of course."

"It'd be better if I sent two of you down there to wrap things up quick," Silas said. "Twig, you up for a couple of days in the saddle?"

"Anything you want, Boss," Twig replied. "So long as when we're done, I can spend an afternoon fishing at Langer's Hole on the company dime."

"You've got yourself a deal," Silas grinned.

Milo cleared his throat. "There's one more angle to this that needs be told."

Silas' eyes narrowed. "Now what?"

"Alf has a sworn affidavit from Judge Rathbone calling for the release of Wes Harms."

Silas sat forward; his lips tight. "Show me the papers."

Alf drew the folded document from his vest pocket and handed it across the desk. Silas studied the it for a long time, reading every line at least twice. When he finished, he sat back with a resigned look. "It all seems in order."

"The man's a menace," Twig said.

"Menace or not, Sturgis is a sworn judge for the State of Kansas," Silas growled. He tossed the papers back to Alf. "Get the cur out of my jail."

Just then, a loud pounding on the door set the men on edge.

"Come in!" Silas yelled.

A young deputy marshal rushed inside; his eyes wide. "Someone robbed the diner!"

The five lawmen were on the run in a flash, arriving at Mother May's Diner in less than three minutes. Twig barely glanced at the dead man near the counter, as his eyes were only for his wife. May Randall stood stoically behind the open cash register. A two-shot derringer sat lazily in one of the drawer slots normally reserved for folding money. One hammer was forward.

Twig stared at her. She stared back unblinking.

"You all right, Ma?" he asked.

"I was closing up for the afternoon," she replied. "He pushed past me before I could lock the door. Showed me a weapon and demanded the cash from the register. I opened it, armed myself, and shot him in the breadbasket. Didn't want to do it, but he had no claim to what I rightly earned."

Twig studied her face, then reached out and gently took her hand in his.

Silas bent down and examined the dead man—his finger still in the trigger of the pistol he never had a chance to use. He studied the angle of the body in relation to both the door and the cash register. Everything aligned with May

69

Randall's story. "Lock the place up, Twig, and take May home. I'll send someone else with Milo to Loess."

Silas motioned, and two men carried the dead man out the back door. May Randall watched the procession stoically.

When they'd gone, Twig asked again. "You all right, Ma?"

"Fit as a fiddle," she relied. "He made the choice, not me."

"I've got business in Loess that'd require me being gone a couple of days. You want me here or you want me to do my job?"

"I'm a big girl," she replied. "My conscience ain't nagging me."

Twig nodded, then turned to Milo. "Get Harms out of lock-up. Take the trail past my place and I'll ride with you from there."

Silas started to speak. "But, Twig…"

Twig's back straightened. "No buts about it, Silas. I've got a job to do and I'm gonna do it. If Ma says she's fine, I, for one, am gonna take her word for it."

May Randall squeezed her husband's hand.

"I'll ride home with her and make sure she's settled in," Twig added. "Then I'll ride south with the fellas. No further discussion necessary."

Silas nodded his agreement and turned to leave; the Loess lawmen close behind him.   Milo faced May. "Thanks again for looking after my place when I was gone, Ma. I sincerely appreciate it. There's just one thing more I'd ask. I've got two puppies who done wiggled their way into my life and I've no means for caring for them while I'm in Loess. You of a mind to look in on 'em?"

The makings of a smile cracked her stoic mask. "You might not get 'em back if I grow attached."

Milo rubbed the stubble on his chin. "There's two of them and two of us. You're too tough to wrassle for 'em, so take your choice and we'll each have some joy in our house."

"Deal," she replied through a full smile.

Milo turned to leave, already dreading his upcoming ride with Wes Harms.

May's voice cut across him. "Just so we're both on the same page, I'd beat you fair and square if we did wrassle. I ain't scared of you."

Milo grinned as he opened the door. "Why do you think I gave up so easily?"

71

The walk from Mother May's Diner back to the Armory was less than a quarter-mile, but it lasted forever in Alf Lemure's mind. Milo Thorne's words took seed in his brain and grew to the point they were pressing against both ears. *Sloppy work...better than that...hung the wrong guy.* Milo stopped at his desk to get his key for the cell door, giving the sheriff more time to think. *Get yourself together, Alf. You've got a job to do. Harms is dangerous even when you're clear-headed.* When they reached the jail, a familiar voice rang clearly in his memory. *A fool's gold friend tells you what you want to hear. Hold close to those who will tell you the truth—even if it's bitter.* Alf paused, his hand on the massive oak door. *No truer words have ever been spoken. You always were a smart man, Pa.* He took a deep breath and followed Milo through the entrance, almost knocking over the man they'd come to see.

"Well, I'll be damned..." A straw-haired turnkey snapped. "Where you going in such a rush, Milo?"

"Sorry, Big Joe. We're coming to see you. This here's Alf Lemure, he's the Sheriff down in Loess."

"I'm glad to know you think I'm worth hurrying about for." He smiled and the two men shook hands. "What stoked the fire under your boots?"

72

"Official business."

The jailer scratched the stubble on his chin. "Well, you're in luck. We're always open."

Milo returned a wan smile. "We're here to spring Wes Harms."

"I'm afraid that'd take a judge's order."

Alf handed over the affidavit from Sturgis Rathbone.

The jailer unfolded the paper and read it slowly. His gaze moved to the Sheriff. "I've known Sturgis for thirty years, and I've always known him to be an honest man. I'll trust him on this, but that don't mean I have to like it."

"I understand," Alf replied. "I don't like it any more than you do."

"Does Silas know?"

"Yes, he already read the affidavit."

"I'm guessing he ain't jumping for joy over this?"

Milo shook his head. "That's an understatement. Twig and I will be riding back to Loess with Harms. I'd appreciate it if you'll bring the scoundrel out to Sheriff Lemure. I've got to get my travel roll from my office."

Milo excused himself, leaving Big Joe alone with the Loess lawmen.

The jailer nodded. "Milo's probably hoping the feral dog makes a run for it."

A smile returned to Alf's face and he shrugged. "That'd definitely make things easier."

Ten minutes later, the Big Joe led a shackled man in a shabby duster coat into the lobby, his blond hair spilling from beneath a black derby partially obscuring a sneer on his lips.

A sour look grew on the man's face when he saw Alf Lemure. "Well, look who's here to save the day. If it isn't the Sheriff of Dust City, himself."

Big Joe ratcheted the handcuffs tighter at the show of disrespect. "Mind your manners, you no-count…"

"That's all right," Alf said. "He can speak his piece. It falls on deaf ears."

Harms twisted free of the jailer's grip. "And a guilty conscience."

When the procession reached the top step of the boardwalk, they found Milo at the hitching post, holding the reins of an unsaddled horse.

When Harms caught sight him, his face reddened. "Well, if it ain't the crippled giant."

Milo handed the reins to Newby and climbed to the top step. "I figured this would be your disposition, mouse." He drew a handkerchief from his pocket and stuffed it into the scoundrel's mouth.

Newby smiled at him. "That should give us some peace and quiet for a stretch."

Alf threw Harms onto the back of the unsaddled horse, removed Big Joe's shackles, and placed his own on the flailing wrists of the prisoner. He handed back the handcuffs and shook the turnkey's hand. "Thanks again, Joe. It was nice meeting you."

"It was good to meet you too, Alf," Big Joe replied. "Next time, I hope it's under better circumstances. I know Sturgis Rathbone and I trust him, but this whole deal smells worse than a wool blanket in the rain. See to it that you steer clear of whatever tempest this demon is stirring up."

Alf said nothing.

Milo read the shame on his face. "Sounds like a familiar refrain."

CHAPTER THIRTEEN

A few miles outside town, Milo and the Loess lawmen made a sharp turn through a dusty rock outcropping and came out onto the property of Twig and May Randall. Twig was mounted up and waiting for them; his horse stepping into pace with nary a missed a beat.

Milo glanced at the house and saw May's stern face in the window watching them pass. He nearly fell from the saddle when she dabbed her eyes with a white handkerchief.

Rod Newby quickened his pace and rode point, while Milo and Twig slid into the drag role. Despite his discomfort, the rocking sway of the saddle had lulled Wes Harms to sleep; however, Alf never dropped his guard. He knew Harms was as dangerous as any man, even with his eyes closed.

After five miles, Milo took in his senior partner, who sat stiffer than normal in the saddle—his eyes straight ahead, as if his mind was anywhere but on the journey. Milo rode abreast and noticed Twig's gaze never wavered.

"You all right there, old-timer?" Milo asked.

"My body's in this saddle, but my head's back at home."

"Ma not want you to go?"

"She wouldn't tell me if she didn't. The woman has sand, Milo. Ne'er a truer soul born of this earth."

"Then what's dragging your heels?"

"Seeing the look in her eye at the diner's got me shook."

"She looked like the same Ma Randall to me," Milo replied.

"I know her better'n I know my own self. Killing that fella cut her deep. You might not have seen it, but I sure 'nuff did."

Milo thought of May's out-of-place tears and he softened. As they rode, he noticed Twig's shoulders sag, something Milo never thought he'd see.

The next words from Twig's mouth were even more of a surprise. "Kansas City's getting too wild," he said to the

77

wind. "Too many hopped up muttonheads. Blame near unsafe."

Stunned at the admission, Milo couldn't muster a response.

Twig finally turned his eyes to his partner. "I worry about Ma. I couldn't stand it if she got hurt." His eyes dropped. "What if that'd have been her on the floor instead of the fool who tried to rob her?"

"She handled herself quite well from what I saw."

Twig shook his head. "I and you are trained in gunplay, Milo. Yet, both of us sport scars from the job. Ma ain't trained as such." His eyes rose again, and Milo saw a hint of something he'd never registered from the warrior that was Twig Randall—fear. "I'm afraid it'll catch up to her someday."

"She's a special woman," Milo said. "I'm alone, so I can't see life from your eyes on this one. I'll go with your instincts."

"My instincts are as frazzled as a treed possum."

Twig's admission was so out of character that Milo's hands clenched on his reins. When Twig spoke again, Milo saw the faintest tremble in his upper lip.

"I don't want my wife to be the one playing dead."

****

When the men had gone, May Randall dried her eyes and poured herself a strong cup of tea. Her emotions were raw and her nerves jangled.

Do something, May.

Her promised chore for Milo came to her. She went to the corral, saddled a mount, and started on the mile-long ride to Milo's ranch. When she opened his front door, her ankles were immediately under attack from the licks of two vicious fur babies.

Despite her day of tribulations, her spirits soared.

"Well, this won't do," she purred. "I can't care for you from a mile away." She picked them up and their thick coats warmed her hands. "Looks like you'll have to come home with me."

****

Wes Harms woke three hours later when they stopped to water the horses. Milo took the rag from his mouth and lowered him from the saddle to stretch his legs. His hands were raw from the pig-iron shackles and his jaw ached.

"Where are we?" he mumbled.

"About half-way back to Loess" Alf answered. "If I were you, I'd keep my wits about me and my mouth shut."

"Why am I shackled? What cause do you have to treat me like an animal? You just wait…"

The talk stopped when Milo stepped back into view. "Comfortable, Harms?"

"Go to hell, Cripple!"

Milo looked up at the vast, barren land that stretched out in all directions. "You know, Alf, there's no witnesses out here. How about you set the varmint free, so I can shoot an escaping prisoner."

"That is one hell of an idea, Milo. I've got the key right here."

Harms didn't say another word until the outskirts of Loess.

CHAPTER FOURTEEN

Sturgis Rathbone sat at his desk going over a new batch of wanted posters when Galen Reid entered his office unannounced. Despite the warmth of the late afternoon, the Judge felt chills run down his spine. "What can I do for you, Mister Reid?"

The pale man tottered on his undersized rachitic legs. "Oh, come, come, *Your Honor*. I think we should be on more familiar terms than that. After all, you have played cards at my residence."

The subtle jab hit its mark. *And you'll never let me forget it either.* "What can I do for you, Galen?"

"Any news from Kansas City?"

"If everything went smoothly, and I have no reason to think it wouldn't, they could be back soon. That is, if Harms cooperated."

The distended face of Galen Reid broke into a grin. "Oh, I'm sure he will be as pleasant as a warm summer's breeze."

Sturgis hesitated, then spoke his piece. "You need to rein that one in, Galen. He's pure trouble. Something bad is going to come to pass if he's allowed to continue his evil ways."

Reid's toady grin faded. "I will do no such thing. Wes is spirited, I'll give you that, but you don't give the orders. It is I who hold the cards here!"

Sturgis stood slowly and turned on Reid. "That is the last time I will be threatened, implied or not. You gave your word."

Reid did not cow. "I see it differently, *Your Honor*. I am a man of great intelligence, and I never forget. Cross me, and I'll see you swing from that infernal tree yourself."

Hatred welled in Sturgis and his fists balled. He took a step toward the monster with malice—until he heard the approaching horses. Reid reacted first, turning for the door as quickly as his girth allowed. Both arrived in the street just in time to see the oddly-arranged delivery party.

Reid saw the shackled body of Wes Harms and gasped. "He's dead!"

A cheerful smile crossed the judge's mouth, yet all hope was dashed when the horses came to a stop in front of them.

Harms wiggled so hard his derby fell off. He yelled to Reid. "Tell them to get me down from here, Galen!"

"Get him down from there, Sturgis." Reid magpied.

When the judge didn't move, Reid charged Milo's horse, spitting demands as he moved, grabbing at the shackled hands of his ward. Caught off-guard, Milo hesitated. When Reid struck him in the leg with his fist, Milo shook it off. But, when Reid slapped Boots' haunches with his walking stick, Milo's anger got the best of him. Reid took two steps back when Milo leapt from his mount. Alf slid from his horse and pulled the shackle key from his pocket. When the lock clicked open, Milo grabbed the scruff of the prisoner's duster and held him out in front of Reid. The boots of Wes Harms were two feet off the ground.

"Is this yours?"

Reid thrust his hands up. "Why, yes, he is."

The big man gave a crooked smile. "Then I'd strongly suggest that you break his childish behaviors. Next time we cross paths, I won't take the time to read any cagey testimonials. I'll turn this rat into a wheel of Swiss cheese."

Unaccustomed to the receiving end of bullying dialogue, Reid's protestation was weak. "Now, see here…you can't…"

He raised his cane toward Milo, but the big man swung his stump, knocking the walking-stick thirty feet down the street, cleaving it in two.

The giant stared down at Reid. "I think I'll decide what I can or can't do, if that suits you."

When Milo lowered Harms to the ground, the ruffian snatched up his derby, slapped it on his head, and started swinging at him. Milo took a feint step towards Harms, who jumped back as if struck by lightning. Milo laughed at the cowardice of the arrogant brat. Harms answered by spitting in Milo's face. Milo grabbed the front of Harms' shirt with his massive right hand, once again lifting him off the ground. Reid began to howl, striking Milo with his ham-like fists. The Marshal twisted and flung Harms down the street, nearly as far as the two halves of Reid's broken, pearl-handled cane. Harms scrambled to his feet and sprinted toward Reid's carriage.

Milo pointed toward the running man with his enormous stump and barked at Galen Reid. "If I see that mongrel around Kansas City again it'll take more than a piece of paper to get him out of trouble. You'll need a broom and a bucket to fetch the smithereens of him. Now, get!"

Reid waddled away as fast as his fat, little feet could shuffle.

Wes Harms hollered at him to run, but Reid was incapable. The lawmen stood by as the fat dandy clumsily piled into the waiting surrey. The mixture of haste and infirmity resulted in Reid not being fully inside the vehicle before Harms whipped the horses. The team lurched forward and Reid was tossed head-over-heels into the back seat of the buggy.

As they drove past the lawmen, Harms took one last parting shot. "This ain't over, cripple!"

Milo Thorne shook his head as the pathetic circus act rolled by. "That one's trouble, Your Honor. First time I ever had to shackle someone to bring him home and set him free."

Sturgis nodded. "He'll be Reid's downfall."

Alf glanced at the Judge. "If not ours."

As the spectacle passed out of sight, Judge Rathbone smiled grimly. He took a deep breath and looked up at the giant. "Howdy, Milo." He then spied Milo's partner. "Howdy, Twig. It's been a while. What brings you south, old friend?"

Twig's smile twisted into a grimace. "It seems that we have a two-headed monster to slay, Your Honor."

Sturgis looked from Twig to Milo; his brow furrowed. "How so?"

The tone of Milo's answer denoted a shift from greeting to business. "Well, it seems like you hung Handsome Hal Hampton a month after I shot him dead in Colorado."

Rathbone swallowed hard and turned his gaze toward the clearing where Widowmaker stood. His mouth dropped. The lawmen followed his gaze.

In the distance, the limbless form of the gnarled oak jutted toward the clouds.

Alf swallowed hard. "Well, I'll be damned."

A wry smile crossed Milo's mouth. "Don't a hanging tree require at least one limb?"

"Don't just stand there, Alf." Sturgis barked. "Get up to the Nob and see what happened."

The Sheriff leapt into action, swinging his leg onto his horse. As quick as he was, Milo beat him to the punch and his horse was already galloping toward the clearing with Twig hot on his tail.

When they arrived, Milo scattered a flock of buzzards who were picking at the bodies, then reined up next to the sheriff. "How many were on the limb, Alf?"

"Four, counting Hampton."

Twig shook his head. "Sturgis has always been prone to the noose, but I only see what's left of three bodies."

The men paused as the Judge rode into the clearing, his face blank as the gruesome scene came into view. The shock of the carnage registered immediately, followed by the raising of a kerchief to ward off the stench.

Milo eyed the magistrate. *This is a man who is used to making judgments, but not familiar with their aftermath.*

Twig moved next to Sturgis and dismounted. "Steady there, Your Honor. We don't need to add another log on the pile."

"There's only three," Sturgis muttered.

"Was the man you called Hampton last on the limb?" Milo asked.

"Yes," Alf replied.

"Then our work here is done."

Alf's gaze turned to Milo. "How's that?"

"We came here to investigate you hanging an innocent fella," Milo grinned. "Seems like you might have given it a go, but unless a ghost can leave tracks, your dead man ran off in quite a hurry."

"How do you figure that?" Sturgis asked.

Milo pointed at the boot prints in the dust with the stump of his left hand. "I submit the evidence, Your Honor."

Alf's voice cut across them. He was twenty yards away, reading the path of the signs. "Are you all done fooling around? We've got an escaped prisoner on the loose."

"You hung him for a murder committed by another person," Twig shot back. "You got something else to pin on him?"

Alf's face flushed.

Sturgis held out his hands. "He's right, Alf. The crime on the wanted poster was the sole reason we hung him."

"The fella who made those tracks wasn't wanted for anything," Milo said. "Hal Hampton was the one we were looking for and he's dead. This one here's a frontier miracle."

Sturgis stared at Milo; confusion covered his face. "Why's that, Milo?"

"He not only died with his boots on," Milo chuckled. "He was resurrected likewise!"

The big marshal boomed out a laugh, but neither the sheriff nor the judge responded in kind. Milo noted their lack of mirth. "Ah, don't be so doggone sullen. An innocent man was given a second chance. The mouse beat the cat for once, so don't be such sourpusses. Come on, let me buy you a drink to wash the dust from your mouth."

Milo swung himself up into his saddle and began whistling a nameless tune. The lawmen of Loess rode in silence behind him.

****

Andy Steele dropped his head below the sill of the barn window when heard a fast-approaching wagon screech to a halt in the yard. The familiar shrill voice of the heavy man who lived in the house yelled, "You drove the horse hard, Wes. You need to care for it."

"You care for it!" a new voice screamed back, then muttered several cuss-words as it retreated, silenced only when the front door slammed in anger. Knowing that the wagon would end up in the barn, Andy burrowed deep into the straw. He heard the heavy man wheezing and grunting as he wiped down the horse and filled its feed trough—muttering under his breath as he worked.

89

Quite the pair, Andy thought. *The new fella sounds like a handful.*

The remainder of the day was uneventful, Andy catching cat-naps on and off. That changed rapidly as night fell. A lamp, lit at dusk in the main quarters, gave off a faint light. Andy could make out movement against a linen window cover. A second light flickered to life in a rear bedroom and loud noises shattered the peace, as if things were being thrown about. When the bedroom light went out, Andy heard the yelling start in the front room.

He sat up, watching with intent. *This might get interesting.*

****

It is a curious thing in life that those who build their personal realms upon false pretenses carry themselves in two distinct, but mutually-exclusive manners: The first is unseeing. An air of ego-driven arrogance shields their vision from those whom they hurt and oppress. Oblivion is peaceful, while the maelstrom that surrounds them remains invisible. The second sees everything. Cautious and fretful, with every interaction viewed as an attempt to wrest away that which they possess.

Paranoia ensues. The pie is not sliced and distributed, but coveted and closely guarded.

Galen Reid fell into the first category. His constant companion, Wes Harms, was the abject definition of the second.

Inside the very house that Andy Steele spied, Galen Reid took a hard line on Wes Harms' misdeeds in Kansas City, but Harms was having none of it. Talk around the table went from a quiet discussion, to an attempted patriarchal lecture, to a full-blown shouting match—all before dinner even hit the table.

During a lull, Reid asked his most pertinent question about Harms' trip north. "You were supposed to pick up a package for me."

"I did."

"May I have it?"

"I opened it."

"Where are the contents?"

Harms' answer was nonchalant. "I spent it."

Reid's face went crimson. "You spent a thousand dollars in one night?"

"What's it to you? You have plenty more. You own the whole damned town."

"That's not the point. I needed that money for expenses. Besides, how can I trust you going forward?"

Harms squared on the older man. "Who says you need to?"

Reid shook his head in defeat. "Oh, Wesley, you'll be the death of me yet."

"May be," Harms sneered. "I can't believe you let those brutes treat me like they did."

"I got you free as soon as I could. It took my considerable wherewithal to make it happen."

"I'm telling you, Uncle Galen, that giant cripple is up to no good. He roughed me up in Kansas City and he shackled me to that horse all the way back here." Harms froze at a noise outside, then moved like a cat to the door. "Who's out there?"

The heavy man's shrill voice could be heard from the house's interior. "Nothing's out there, Wes. Probably an animal. Come back inside."

"It's probably that big marshal spying on me."

"Don't think like that."

"Don't tell me how to think. You don't know that monster!"

Rough footsteps and a slamming door echoed in the night. The yard plunged back into darkness.

CHAPTER FIFTEEN

The Irishman was the main social gathering point of Loess. Large enough to house a faro table and a small stage, and modern enough to serve both warm beer and whiskey, it drew a respectable clientele. Directly next door was the Broken Shoe, which was smaller, darker, and more nefarious than its competition. The Shoe held only a bar, no tables, and offered a menu consisting of a single item—whiskey. The locals knew the Shoe as simply a place to stop for false courage before going upstairs to the bordello. To the locals, it was a well-known fact that both establishments were owned by the same man—Galen Reid.

Ryan Muldoon stood behind the mahogany counter of The Irishman cleaning out a shot glass when the massive form of Milo Thorne stepped through the front door. Anticipating trouble from the dark-clad stranger, Muldoon reached under the counter for his blackjack. His grip on the weapon eased as he saw Sturgis Rathbone, Alf Lemure and Rod Newby follow the big man into the room. A fifth man, slight but steely-eyed was last to enter. The Judge waved at the bartender and the five men sat at an empty table near the back of the saloon.

"Evening, Muldoon."

"Evening, Judge." The man nodded toward Sturgis and then turned. "Evening, Sheriff."

"Howdy, Muldoon." Lemure pointed toward their guest. "This here is Milo Thorne and Twig Randall, they're Kansas Marshals. You already know the Mute."

"Evening, fellas."

The giant doffed his cap. "I prefer to be on good terms with the men who I do business with. I'd be honored if you'd called me Milo."

Muldoon smiled. "Welcome, Milo. My name's Ryan."

"Evening, Ryan. We're in town on official business, searching for some missing property."

Muldoon straightened. "I'll help as much as I can. What was took?"

Milo swung his left arm up and slammed his stump on the table. "It was pinkish and had five wiggly things attached to it."

Muldoon jumped back and gasped. Milo let out a howl of laughter that was instantly joined by the lawmen. Muldoon gathered himself and chuckled. "Oh, I can tell that you are a live group. Whiskey or beer?"

Sturgis glowered at the barkeep. "Are we men, or horses?" He could not stop the corners of his mouth creeping upward.

Muldoon smiled back. "Whiskey it is."

Judge Rathbone leaned forward. "Might as well bring the whole bottle, Ryan. We haven't seen each other in quite a piece."

Milo grabbed Muldoon's arm. "Make mine sarsaparilla, Ryan."

The other men froze.

"You feeling all right?" Twig asked.

"Sound of body and mind," Milo replied. "Ever since I swore off the spirits."

Muldoon glanced at the resolve on Milo's face and realized he wasn't kidding. He then glanced at Sturgis who shrugged his shoulders.

"Sarsaparilla it is," the barkeep muttered. "Might take a minute, as I'll need to send someone to the dry goods store after it."

Milo nodded. "I've got nothing but time."

The men settled in for the evening and the conversation flowed freely. Muldoon was sent to the hotel for five steak dinners, which he agreed to happily, as it turned out Marshal Thorne was a generous tipper.

Halfway through their dinner, Sturgis asked the question that had been festering in the back of his brain. "Say, Milo, what was Harms in jail for in Kansas City?"

"He stabbed one of the painted ladies from the Hot Top Saloon."

Sturgis blanched. "Did she die?"

Twig shook his head. "If it weren't for Doc Morris, she would have."

Milo turned in his chair. "He's a bad seed, Sturgis. He'll end up killing eventually. He's fighting some serious demons inside that pea-brain of his." He saw the heads of both

96

the Judge and the Sheriff fall forward. "Has Harms got something on the two of you?"

Neither man moved.

The silence was interrupted by Muldoon. "You fellas want another round?"

"Yes, Ryan," Twig answered. "Thank you."

Milo glared at his drinking partners. "Forget I asked the last. Your silence answered my question."

Sturgis raised his eyes to the big man's. "We'll get around to it eventually. Needless to say, neither of us are all too keen on him."

Milo nodded. "Understood." He glanced at Newby and noticed the dejected look on his face. "What's bothering you, Rod?"

"I thought I was in tall clover. Hampton's reward was five-hundred dollars."

Milo drew out a thick wad of folding money and snapped off a few bills. "I'll split it with you, half and half. Here's two-fifty."

Newby's eyes bulged when the marshal handed him the cash. "But, Milo, I can't…"

"Next topic," was the big man's terse reply.

Familiar with Milo's tendency to give away reward money, Twig grinned and shook his head.

"Milo, there's been something I've been meaning to ask you," Alf chimed in.

"Fire away."

"What the hell is a golem?"

Milo chuckled. "A golem is from ancient Jewish folklore. It's a being made of earth magically brought to life."

Alf's brow tightened. "How the hell do you know these things?"

"You want the long version or the short?"

"Let's go with the long," Alf smiled.

"Well, seeing as how you two ain't sharing your story, we have ample time for mine. In another lifetime, my father wanted me to become a man of letters—a great lawyer. He used his influence to get me admitted to one of our nation's institutions of higher learning."

Sturgis laid down his fork. "University of Missouri?"

Milo smiled. "No. Harvard University."

The Judge nodded, impressed.

Alf had a blank look on his face. "Where's that?"

"Near Boston."

Sturgis regarded the Marshal with newfound respect. "Did you finish?"

"Yes, sir. I did. I moved back to Vermont to hang my shingle."

"How did you end up in Kansas?" Alf asked.

"My father up and died on me. He wrote in his will that he wanted me to see this magnificent country of ours. On my travels, I met Silas Petit and Twig here in Kansas City and found my direction in life. Been there ever since. I enjoy the challenges of being a lawman; the excitement, and the feeling of doing something honorable with my life." He leaned back in his chair and drained the last of his sarsaparilla. "Plus, I enjoy an occasional scrap."

The big man smiled and glanced to his left. He saw a smile on the face of the Sheriff and noticed his head nodding. "You too, Alf?"

"Couldn't have said it better myself."

Muldoon brought another round of whiskey and the men relaxed into a post-dinner melancholy. After several minutes of silence, Muldoon returned to pick up the empty glasses from the table. He paused before leaving and muttered a question into the void.

"How did you lose your hand, Milo?"

Alf and Sturgis tensed at the coarse inquiry. Muldoon noticed their reaction and quailed as the giant turned to face him. He didn't see the impish smile on Twig Randall's mouth.

"Well, no one has had the nerve to ask me that in quite some time, Mister Muldoon."

"I'm sorry, Marshal. I meant nothing by it."

The Marshal fixed the barkeep with a stare. "It seems I was at the altar. My beautiful bride placed the ring on my index finger and I started dying from that digit upward. The preacher had the wits to chop off my hand to stop the curse from spreading."

Muldoon's face morphed from terror to hilarity as Milo burst into laughter. Sturgis and Alf mustered the courage to draw their first breaths since the original question was lobbed. Both Twig and Rod Newby shook with fits of the giggles.

Muldoon sighed. "Doesn't it make it hard to be a lawman?"

"It's harder to work without wits than it is without a left hand. I get by. If I can't beat them in a fight, I just shoot them."

The barkeep's eyes widened. "Killed a lot of men?"

Milo looked at him with a smile. "Haven't met one yet that could beat me in a fight."

Muldoon laughed and placed a round of full glasses on the table. "These are on me. Thanks for not killing me for the question, Marshal."

Milo raised his sarsaparilla in a toast. "Here's to swimmin' with bow-legged women."

CHAPTER SIXTEEN

The next morning, Milo, Twig, and Alf saddled up for the most important task of any lawman's trip south to Loess—fishing at Langer's Hole. Known for miles around as the most abundant source for big trout in the entire State of Kansas, the Hole rarely disappointed. A bit over a mile outside Loess, along the confluence of a narrow river and a meandering stream, the Hole was a jewel, and the trail that led there went through some of the prettiest land the country had to offer. On the ride out, the three men relaxed in conversation, laughing as they recalled funny stories from their shared profession. As they topped out over a stunted rise, a sturdy farmhouse came into view, surrounded by acres of fallow land.

"Shame to see such a place go to waste," Twig said. "A man could make a fine home there."

Alf glanced at Milo, who said nothing. When they reached the Hole, Twig wet his line and had a fish on before Milo or Alf even baited their hooks.

"The fish don't bite a tarrying worm," Twig chuckled as he landed a four-pounder.

"Throw that one back and catch his daddy," Alf replied. "That's just a baby."

"We'll cook him up for lunch," Twig shot back. "And take the big'uns back for supper."

Two hours later, Twig landed his fifth big fish. He laid his pole on the bank, next to a sleeping Alf Lemure, and sat in the shade—the joy of contentment on his face. "A man could get used to this."

"Fishing?" Milo asked.

"No, slowing down."

"The Twig Randall I know never slows down."

"The Twig Randall I know," said Twig Randall, "has sore knees and a deaf left ear."

Having never heard the man complain, Milo gave him a side-eye.

"And dreams," Twig muttered.

Milo sat up full. "Dreams?'

"Dreams of a place where it ain't so crowded…" Twig paused. "And where May is safe."

"I said before, she can care for herself."

"I don't want her to have to," Twig replied. "If Kansas City gets any more dangerous, they'll have to issue guns to the cows so they can make it as far as the stockyards."

Bewildered by Twig's position, Milo asked his next question with moderate consternation. "So, what are you talking about here?"

"Selling my spread and the diner and buying that land we passed on the way here."

A single word echoed from under Alf's hat. "Can't."

Twig's eyebrows cocked. "What'd you say?"

Alf took the hat off his face and sat up. "You can't. That place sold last year."

"And it's still fallow?" Twig asked. "Who bought it?"

Milo said nothing.

Alf cleared his throat. "According to Sam McLaren, Milo did."

Twig's stare shot to his partner. "That so?"

"Yep."

"Why didn't you tell me?"

Milo pulled a blade of grass off the bank and put it in his mouth. "It's not for me."

"Quit dancing around," Twig said. "Take a deep breath and spill your guts."

"You remember the three brothers who got mixed up with Johnny McAlister a while back?"

"What about 'em?"

"That spread's theirs."

Twig scratched his ear. "As I recall, two of 'em are dead."

"And one isn't," Milo replied. "The place is not for sale."

Alf picked up a pebble and tossed it in the river. "And Galen Reid's got a stranglehold on the remaining land around here."

"That's who I bought the property from," Milo chuckled. "Thought he'd out-foxed me, but it turns out the quicker fox only has one paw."

"Huh, bought it for someone else." Twig shook his head. "You and your giving nature. There's no softer touch around."

Alf shrugged. "It's an endearin' quality."

"His only one." Twig's head was still shaking. "You remember that story of the fella who died from a spear in the heel?"

"I 'member the tale, but not his name," Alf replied.

"Achilles," Milo muttered.

"That's the fella," Twig said. "That big 'ol heart is your Achille's Heel. Surprised you didn't give these fish a fresh worm and toss 'em back to the deep."

"I like seeing folks happy," Milo replied. "What's so odd about that? Makes me feel good to help someone else feel good."

"Well, I want to be happy, and more important, I want my wife to be happy," Twig sighed. "So, I'm fixin' to scout around."

"You aren't going anywhere," Milo shot back.

The humor blinked out of Twig's eyes. "Yes, Milo, I am. I want my wife to die of old age in a rocking chair, not have her snuffed out by some smelly cowboy who spent a month's wages getting' boozed up and didn't like the way the diner served his eggs."

Milo sat back and stared to the heavens. "I just got back from a month away and everything is changing. Paula's gone and now you're fixing to leave." He sat up and looked at

Twig. "I already lost my hand, my future wife, and now my friend?" The words, *it just isn't fair* formed on his tongue, but he swallowed them. He took a steadying breath. "This is a tough one to accept."

Twig's brow furrowed. "You don't want Ma and I to be happy?"

"Of course," Milo paused, "I just don't want my life to change…" He flinched at the words coming out of his own mouth. *What have you become, you selfish brat?* He forced his voice back to even. "When are we talking about?"

Twig hesitated, but when he spoke his voice was stern with resolve. "As soon as I find a proper setting."

Twig picked up his stringer of trout and went down to the river's edge to clean them. Milo sat still on the bank, struggling to get air to his heavy heart.

****

Never one to be cowed, Wes Harms strutted down Main Street, purposefully failing to notice the people giggling about the spectacle of the past day. When he reached the southern end of town, he ducked into the Broken Shoe and paused to let his eyes adjust to the darkness. He caught glimpses of movement and wisps of faint perfume, but heard nothing.

107

When the bar finally blinked into view, Harms spotted the familiar form of Spike Duggan wiping down glasses.

"Afternoon, Spike."

"Wes."

"Gimme a whiskey."

The big man poured a jigger full and Harms drank it in one gulp. "Another."

Duggan nodded. "All right, but two's your limit."

Even in the faint light, the flush was visible on Harms' cheeks. "Says who?"

"Orders from Galen himself."

The back door slammed and Harms flinched. Duggan chuckled at the reaction.

"Damn him to hell," Harms spat. "I'll drink as much as I want."

Duggan reached below the bar and produced a thick billystick, sitting on the sink behind him. "Orders are orders."

"I'll have your job for this."

Duggan flexed his thick muscles and picked up the club. "Not 'til I take it out of your hide first."

Harms seethed. "Give me the drink."

Duggan poured another jigger and slid it across the bar.

Harms gulped it down and wiped his lips. "Where's Trixie?"

"Out."

"Doris?"

"All of 'em are out."

"Someone was here. I smelled them when I came in."

Duggan shook his head. "They're all out."

Harms lunged at the whiskey bottle, only to have Duggan slap his hand away.

"What is this, Spike? No whiskey and no women? How's Galen supposed to make money?"

Duggan chuckled. "Oh, there's plenty of both—just not for you."

Harms balled his fists, his face twisted in rage. "What's this all about?"

"When you drink," Duggan replied, "you tear the place up and treat the women like animals. No one comes in here anymore for liquor, and the girls are too beat up to see regular customers. That's what makes it difficult for Reid to make money."

Harms lunged for the billy, but the bartender beat him to it. Duggan smacked the back of Harms' arm, sending the smaller man howling in pain toward the door.

"You haven't heard the end of this, Spike!"

As he pushed out onto the street, Harms ran headlong into Jeb Thompson.

"Hey, Wes, where you going in such a hurry?"

"I'm gonna go kill my uncle."

"Good," Thompson snarled. "I'll kill the sheriff at the same time and we'll run the joint."

Harms stared at the big deputy. Neither of the men were smiling.

CHAPTER SEVENTEEN

That evening, Wes Harms hastily lit the stove and threw a floured chicken into a greasy frying pan. As the bird sizzled, Harms rubbed the back of his arm and seethed at Spike Duggan, at Milo Thorne, at life—but, mostly at Galen Reid.

"What's this about limits on me drinking at the Broken Shoe?"

Reid sat at the ornate table that filled the dining room. The stout wooden chair groaned under his weight. "Simple economics. You cost more than the Shoe takes in."

"I want that bastard bartender fired."

"Spike? No, he's harmless."

Harms' eyes narrowed. "He hit me with a club today!"

Reid looked up at his nephew with a half-smile. "Did you deserve it?"

Harms took a step forward, but the hiss of the frying chicken called him back.

"What is this, Uncle Galen? I go away for a week and when I return the world's against me."

"The world's not against you, Wes. But sometimes you've got to adjust to the world."

"You don't."

"Well, I'm me. I own my world."

Harms seethed. "Why should I bend for the world? The world should bend for me. I didn't ask to be born into it. Life owes me more!"

Having never seen him rage as such, Reid stared at his nephew.

Harms forked the chicken onto a plate, the oil spitting and hissing—much like the firebrand who'd heated it. Something moved in the yard. Harms peered out the kitchen window, his face twisted in rage. "I know someone is in the yard, watching me."

"Enough, Wes. No one's out there. Can you finish making our supper? I'm starving."

Harms spun and the carving knife flashed in hand. "Dammit, Galen. All you think about is food and money."

"Dinner I can do without. The money will become an issue between us."

"No loss, like you said, you own the whole damned town."

"Not exactly," Reid sneered. "That money was from my mother's estate. It was to cover the taxes on the Loess property. Now that you've spent it, it's likely to go in arrears. If it does, you'll be asked to find a job, or worse yet, you'll be asked to leave."

Harms slammed the point of the knife into the polished wood of the table, where it wobbled from the force. He took a step forward.

"Please don't do that, Wes. It frightens me."

"I don't care if you mess your small clothes, Galen. You've no right to question my decisions."

Reid put his hands out to shield himself from the approaching menace. "Wes, please—stop!"

Fury raged in the younger man. He stared at the cretin who controlled his entire life. "Why should I?"

"Wes—ple…" Sensing the anger in his nephew's voice, Reid threw up his hands.

Harms struck him hard in the mouth with his right hand. Blood splattered onto the table, spotting the blade of the knife. He leaned in close, their noses almost touching. "Why should I listen to a word you say, you broken down, fat piece of—"

He stuck again, this time with his left. Reid's head jerked violently, his shoulders slumped and he began to weep.

Harms spat on the crying man. "Weak-assed bawler." He slammed his fist against his temple and the fat man went silent. Harms reached into his uncle's jacket and grabbed his over-stuffed wallet, removed a thick wad of cash, and threw the empty shell back into the now unconscious man's face. He walked into the kitchen and drew three pieces of kindling from the stove's wood pile.

"I'm going to cook the fat pig," he mumbled to himself.

Harms stuck the ends of sticks into the roaring oven, waiting impatiently for them to catch fire. When they were ablaze, he snatched out two and moved into the study. He placed one on the bookshelf, watching the flames slowly engulf a thick tome and then spread throughout Reid's impressive library. From there he moved with purpose to the master bedroom, tossing the last torch onto his uncle's overstuffed feather bed. It ignited immediately. Harms sneered at his work, then ran into his own room, returning to the kitchen with a lock-box chocked full of his personal belongings. With great caution, he withdrew the remaining shard of flaming tinder and tossed it into the grease collector at the corner of the kitchen. Flames immediately licked up the wall.

"Cook, piggy!"

Harms donned his derby, gathered his belongings, and fled out the back door.

CHAPTER EIGHTEEN

"Last round, fellas," Ryan Muldoon called. "Closing time."

Milo stared up at him. "Fair enough, Ryan. I'm about full, as it is."

Gunfire erupted on the street outside, followed by loud shouts. The lawmen jumped to their feet and bolted out into the night.

"Fire!"

Realizing that the gun shots were only to draw attention, Alf turned his gaze toward the flames. "Everybody grab a bucket! Form a human chain. Now!" When no one responded, he resorted to the Old West announcement method—drawing his six-shooter and firing a single shot into the air. The mob quieted. "Grab a bucket and form a chain.

Let's get some water on it!" As the crowd jumped into action, Alf set a course for the source of the flames. As he hit the edge of town, realization set in. *That's Galen Reid's place.* He spurred his horse hard.

****

Andy Steele heard the approaching horses first. He moved slowly to the open window of the barn to discern who was coming. His eyes glimpsed the orange outlines of the fire one heartbeat before his nose filled with the acrid odor of smoke. *The house!* Fear dug into him. *I hope it doesn't jump to the barn.* He chanced a peek into the yard and froze. *The Sheriff!*

Andy went back into hiding and silently began to pray.

****

Alf reined his horse from a gallop, leapt from its back before it came to a full stop, and ran for the house. From the corner of his eye he saw Harms open the back door and slink toward the barn. *He ain't trying to put it out.* His mind raced. *He set it!*

"Stop right there, Wes!"

Alf bolted after Harms, who turned.

"The barn's next!" Harms slammed the door behind him.

Alf slowed as he reached the building, drew his weapon and took a deep breath. *I didn't see a gun, but that don't mean he ain't got one. Take it slow.* The instant his hand touched the latch, someone yelled his name. He turned and saw Milo leading the townspeople onto the grounds.

"Where you going, Alf?" The big marshal called to him.

Alf pointed to the barn. "Harms!"

Milo caught Twig's attention. "I'll go with Alf; you supervise the bucket brigade. Get some water going. Make it fast!" He dismounted and started running. His first step coincided with the closing of the door behind Sheriff Alf Lemure.

Unarmed, but familiar with the barn's interior, Harms set a plan in motion. He picked up a shoeing hammer and stepped into the shadows. Alf paused for a split-second, then stepped with caution toward the corral side of the barn.

It was the last decision he ever made.

Harms swung the heavy hammer, striking the lawman hard across his right temple. Alf collapsed unabated. Harms rolled the body over, drew the gun from the lawman's holster, and shot him point blank between the eyes. Satisfied the Alf was dead, he stepped back into the shadows.

The door opened and the darkness was pierced by the light of the burning house. Milo stepped inside, using the ambient light to scan the building's interior. The body on the ground was the first thing he saw.

Alf!

He slid the latch back into place and the interior was once again bathed in semi-darkness. Small cracks in the poorly constructed building provided fingers of glowing orange light for illumination. Milo drew his gun and moved toward his fallen friend. As he bent to check the body, cold steel touched the side of his neck.

"You breathe, you're dead," Harms hissed at him. "Let your gun fall to the floor."

Knowing Harms wouldn't hesitate to kill him, Milo's gun clunked to the ground.

"Now, very slowly, stand up and move away from the wall," Harms whispered.

At that moment, the opposite side of the barn erupted in flames, the dry hay providing ample fuel. Milo slowly backed away from Alf's body, stopping beneath the sturdy loft.

"Imagine that, I killed the fool with his own gun." Harm's chuckled. Reflections of flames danced in his eyes.

"Serves the idiot right. You want to hear something funny, Thorne? I used the same gun to kill that punk, Clancy Walker." Harms heard a noise from the hayloft. Not wanting to take his eyes off the giant, he played it off as mice. "The moron thought he could come into my uncle's house and take my money. He was just as big a fool as them other two."

"How'd you trick them?"

"The idiot judge passed out and Lemure wasn't far behind. Walker started taking all our money. I couldn't catch his method, but I knew he was cheating. So, I turned the table over on him. Once he picked himself up, he wanted to fight. I grabbed Lemure's gun and shot him." Harms gave a wicked laugh. "Then I put the gun back in the Sheriff's holster and played it off on the tin star lamebrain." Harms looked at the broken body of Alf Lemure and smiled.

"Did you start the fire?" Milo asked.

"Oh, yeah. I killed that fat bastard uncle of mine and lit the place on fire to cook him."

Milo knew the time was short, but the confession outweighed his concern. "Why are you telling me all this?"

"Who're you going to squeal to? I'm going to use the same damn gun to kill you." Harms pointed Alf's pistol at Milo's chest. "This is going to be so much fu—"

Harms never finished the word. A boot caught him in the back and he crashed forward into Milo. Both men tumbled to the ground and Alf's gun flew into the folds of hay. Milo looked up, but the smoke obscured his vision. He picked up his own pistol, grabbed the body next to Harms' derby and dragged him toward the door. As he neared the door, the opposite loft collapsed, sending fiery remnants everywhere. Milo heard scuttling but the flames drove him toward safety.

When they reached fresh air outside, Milo threw the limp body to the ground and yelled at Twig. "Take care of Harms. There's someone else inside."

Milo sprinted into the burning barn, but the intense heat drove him back. Once outside, he saw Twig administering to the man on the ground.

Twig looked up with a confused look on his face and pointed at his now conscious patient. "This here ain't Harms."

The young man sat up and Milo's jaw went slack. "I—I shot you." He swallowed hard. "Buried you in a dump."

"That wasn't me. I'm not Hal Hampton! My name's Andy Steele. That man, inside, he waylaid the sheriff."

Flames erupted from both sides of the barn. Andy Steele scrambled to his feet and disappeared into the inferno.

Seconds later he stumbled back through the door, dragging the lifeless body of Alf Lemure.

"Why'd you go and do a blame fool thing like that?" Twig asked him.

"Even though he gave plenty of cause to hate him," Andy answered. "My conscience couldn't let him burn."

Milo bent and examined Alf's neck for a pulse. "He's dead."

Just then, the barn collapsed into a heap of flames.

"Anyone in there's dead," Twig added.

"Harms was in there," Milo muttered.

Twig shook his head. "Good riddance."

"He killed Alf," Milo said. "With his own gun."

"Same gun he used to kill my cousin," Andy added.

"Clancy Walker was your cousin?"

"Yes, sir. We rode north together from Waco."

Shouts reverberated through the silence. Milo returned to his senses. "Nothing more we can do for Alf. Let's help with that fire."

Sturgis stood in the yard, barking orders. He glanced to his right when Milo skidded to a stop next to him. "I don't think we can stop it!"

"I hate to be the bearer of bad news, Sturgis, but Alf is dead."

The Judge's stern face softened and his shoulders slumped. Milo reached out to steady him. The movement of the big man's body brought Andy into view.

Sturgis stiffened. "We hung you!"

Milo gripped the Judge's arm. "It's a long story, Sturgis, but trust me, he ain't a ghost." Milo pointed to the human chain and the Judge resumed barking orders. The back door of the house opened and Galen Reid stepped onto the porch.

"Get out of there, Galen!" Sturgis barked.

Reid wobbled, then cried out. "Where's Wes?"

"Harms is dead!" Milo yelled.

"No, he's not!" Reid's eyes widened. "Go to hell, you liar!" He stepped back into the house and latched the door.

"He's in a daze," Sturgis yelled. "We've got to save him!"

Suddenly, a shot rang out from inside, the bullet ripping through the thin walls, striking a wagon near where Milo stood. A second shot was followed by a third in rapid succession. In an instant, bullets flew at a breakneck. Everyone fighting the fire scrambled for cover.

Andy stood transfixed, staring toward the house. "Why's he shooting at us? We're trying to save the ungrateful—"

Milo yanked Andy to safety.

"He's shooting at us!" Andy yelled.

"No," Sturgis answered. "Reid doesn't know how to handle a gun."

"It's bullets cooking off in the house," Twig called. "They'll all fire at once from the heat. Wait till there's a pause and we'll be clear to move."

At the first lull, Milo stood. "You all stay put. I've got an idea." He high-tailed it for the front door, barreling through it with ease. Flames licked across the ceiling and a thick layer of smoke held steady at shoulder height. Milo faltered when he heard the distinctive sound of a heavy body hitting the hardwood floor. He paused to get his bearings and someone ran square into his back. He turned to see Andy behind him.

"You go that way!" Milo pointed. "Stay low, and holler if you find the fat man."

Less than a minute later, the two men bolted from the flaming house, coughing and gasping for air. At that same moment, the roof of the library collapsed. Milo laid Reid's

124

limp body onto the hardpan yard. Andy grabbed his wrist to find a pulse. Twig and Sturgis stepped in close.

Andy offered a faint smile. "He's alive."

Milo turned to the Judge. "Harms set the fire to kill Reid. He murdered Alf." He took two deep breaths to catch his wind. "He also admitted framing you for the murder of Clancy Walker after he shot him with Alf's gun."

The Judge's lips thinned. "He told you all this?"

"Yes, sir. Me and young Mister Steele here." Milo stepped back and put his hand on Andy's shoulder.

Sturgis shook his head at the man who escaped Widowmaker. "How the hell did you…"

A grin crossed Milo's mouth. "It seems as if he survived me shooting him, you hanging him, and Harms burning him up. Hearty stock if you ask me."

Just then, the last standing portion of the house collapsed upon itself. Flames roared and sparks showered the lawn, illuminating the body of Alf Lemure.

"He was a hell of a lawman and friend," Sturgis said. "He'll be sorely missed around these parts."

Milo clapped the Judge on the shoulder. "The last thing Alf would have wanted was us fretting over him. He died doing what he loved."

Sturgis paused in thought, then nodded. "I guess we'll be needing a new sheriff."

Twig stepped to the forefront. "I think I might know just the man."

The remainder of that night was spent tying up loose ends. Alf Lemure's body was taken by wagon to the local undertaker's office, while Galen Reid was transported to one of his hotels where the doctor could see after him. As a group, the lawmen ordered Sturgis to go home, as he was older and had suffered the loss of his best friend. The lawmen and Andy Steele stayed behind to assist the townspeople in mop-up duties. Andy worked tirelessly—half out of a sense of duty, and half because he was now free again to make his own choices.

CHAPTER NINETEEN

The next morning, life marched on, not pausing a beat for the loss of anyone—not even a lawman the quality of Alf Lemure. After his first-ever night's sleep in a hotel bed, courtesy of Milo, Andy settled in over a full breakfast in the hotel cafe.

Milo moseyed down the stairs and pulled up a chair. "Company?"

"Have a seat and tuck in."

After a few bites of hotcakes, Milo cleared his throat. "I'm sorry I haven't had a chance to express my condolences for your cousin. Were you two close?"

"His mother passed when he was a baby. My Mama raised him on account that Clancy was her sister's son. We were like brothers. Clancy came north from Texas to follow his crazy dreams, and I came north to follow Clancy."

"Crazy dreams? How so?"

"I'm two years older than he was. I went to Baylor University down in Waco. Clancy joined me there in my junior year. When I graduated, he said he'd had enough learning. He was good with numbers, and wanted to ride up to St. Louis to start a gambling career on a riverboat. We made it as far as Loess. The blame fool got himself killed for being too good for a small-town poker game, and I got strung up for a murder I didn't commit."

"You graduated from Baylor?"

"Yes, sir. A lot of good it did me."

"What did you study?"

"Education."

Milo nodded. "Plan to teach someday?"

"That was my father's dream for me."

"Is it yours?"

Andy sat his fork on his plate. "My Pa died in my freshman year. Got his head stoved in by a bucking horse. The dream died with him."

"The dream might have perished," Milo mused. "But the knowledge of how to learn will serve a man no matter what path he chooses in life."

"You're right, Marshal," Andy pondered. "Never saw it from that perspective. Opens up the world to new possibilities."

"Where are you headed from here?"

"Home to Texas, I suppose." Andy paused. "But, there's really nothing there for me anymore. Mama remarried six months ago and I don't get along with her new beau."

Twig approached their table, his face business-stern. "Milo, I'd ask you to ride back to Kansas City as soon as you're able. Let Silas know what's happened. I'll stay on down here until things get sorted out."

"As Sheriff?" Milo asked sheepishly.

"Acting only," Twig replied. "None of the men they've got left fit the bill."

"Jeb Thompson?"

"He ain't qualified to lead no one," Twig answered. "He's got more questions than answers, and his questions aren't that of a true lawman."

"How about Shanks or the Mute?"

"Neither wants the job, told me so themselves."

Milo nodded with resignation.

"I'd be happy to help, Mister Randall," Andy chimed in. "I lack a horse, but I've got gumption."

"Andy here's a college graduate," Milo bragged.

"I'll try not to hold that against him," Twig joked. He thought for a moment. "Alf's horse is available. He won't need it and he had no family to speak of. It's yours if you want."

"I was planning on asking Milo if he wanted company on his ride north, but I'd be happy to stick around."

Milo paid the bill and stood. "I covered for your room and board for a month. Lay low here and help Twig sort things out. I'll be back before long."

Andy smiled. "Much obliged, Marshal. I could use some rest. That bed was mighty comfortable."

As he prepared to leave, Twig pulled Milo aside. "I've a favor to ask."

Milo's ears perked.

"Tell Ma I'm sorry, but duty calls. I'll get news to her as soon as things clear up down here."

"Will do."

Twig's eyes dropped. "And, Milo, can you check in with her periodically. I'm a bit worried of her state of mind."

"Say no more. I've got things covered."

Twig turned to leave, but Milo caught him flat-footed. "You don't aim to ever go back, do you?"

Twig spun on his heels and disappeared through the swinging doors into the sunlight.

"Answer received," Milo muttered to no one in particular.

CHAPTER TWENTY

Jeb Thompson lay sprawled on the threadbare couch in his meager front room. A whiskey bottle and a glass sat on a rickety table near his outstretched hand—the only thing either held was memories. Thompson's chest rose and fell in shallow rhythm; his thick snores sending even the cockroaches into hiding. It was a wonder that the knock woke him. Thompson sat up, searching for a time and place to anchor his thoughts. Another loud bang sent him to the coat tree for his gun rig.

"Who's out there?"

"Let me in dammit!"

Thompson's mind whirled; the ground seemed jellified beneath his feet. Another loud bang filled the room. Thompson drew his weapon and jerked open the door.

He immediately retreated four steps while firing willy-nilly at an apparition. "Be gone, ghost!"

The so-called ghost darted for the safety of the jamb. "What are you doing, fool? It's me!"

"You're dead!"

Wes Harms stepped fully into the opening, decked head-to-toe in baggy clothes, topped by a black derby hat with a scorched hawk feather in its band. "I'm not dead, you dolt. It's me!"

Thompson lowered his weapon, his mouth agape.

Harms closed the door. His nose curled at the stench. "Woo wee, someone die in here?"

"You're the one who's dead."

Harms shook his head. "Nope, I made it out. My hat got singed, and my clothes ruined, but I'm in one piece."

"Where'd you get those clothes?"

"Remember the man who lived on the old Porter place? They're his. He doesn't need them anymore."

"Why's that?"

"He's dead."

Thompson's eyes narrowed. "You killed him for his clothes?"

"Mine got ruined in the fire. I needed new ones. I can't go around in nothing but my hat," Harms quipped. "Even a ghost needs clothes."

Thompson blinked several times in rapid succession. "Galen know you made it out?"

"No one knows."

Thompson put his gun away. "Well, I'm glad you're alive."

"It's better if I stay dead." A smirk crossed his face. "It'll make us both rich."

"Huh?" Thompson shook the cobwebs out of his head. "Without Galen, you ain't got a pot to piss in."

"If I'm dead, no one'll be expecting me," Harms sneered. "It was a flesh and bone Wes Harms who killed that lout sheriff, but it'll be a ghost Wes Harms who kills every damned one of them still alive—Spike Duggan, that big bastard of a marshal, and anyone else who gets in the way. We'll take Loess, you and I."

Thompson's brain cleared slightly. "What about Galen?"

"Aw, we're kin. He'll likely forgive me. Always has."

"I don't know, Wes. He's all fired upset."

"You've known me since we were knee-high to a grasshopper, Jeb. How many times has the fat fool let me off with a slap on the wrist?"

"Every time," Thompson chuckled. "But what if this time's different?"

"Then, like I said, I'll kill him and we'll run the town. We'll be rolling in the dough."

"The new sheriff?"

A wicked smile crossed the mouth of Wes Harms. "I'll leave him to you."

CHAPTER TWENTY-ONE

When Milo reached Kansas City the next day, he noticed two heavily-laden wagons parked on the street. His eyes narrowed in familiarity, yet he couldn't recall where he'd seen them— that is until he saw a stout-framed man with dark hair standing on the raised boardwalk in front of the Armory.

Newt Brand took off his hat and smiled. "Howdy, Milo."

"Howdy right back at you," Milo replied through a grin. "You made decent time."

"You beat us here, and we left Monroe a day before you."

"True, but it was just Boots and I. A man travels fast when he travels light."

"What can I say?" Newt chuckled. "Mags is a taskmaster, stopped only when necessary."

As if on cue, Maggie Brand sauntered out of the dry goods store, her steps both sure and graceful. She beamed when she saw Milo. "Well aren't you a sight for sore eyes."

"Newt says this is the first time you've stopped since you left Colorado," Milo laughed.

Maggie pulled a pin from her tight bun, and shook out her auburn hair. "He's getting old. Needed to stop every ten minutes to empty his bladder."

"Maggie, please!"

Milo laughed at Newt's suddenly red face.

"Where's the newlyweds?" Milo asked.

"They're wandering around," Maggie replied. "First time either's been in a city of this size. They'll likely get lost."

"Hopefully they get back before breakfast," Newt rubbed his belly. "I'm starving."

"I know just the place," Milo replied. "I've got to deliver a message to the owner."

As they crossed the street to Mother May's Diner, Jacob and Sara Brand walked hand-in-hand down the sidewalk toward them. The strapping young man shook Milo's hand, while his supple, blonde-haired wife engulfed the marshal in a

137

hug. Once the hellos were said, Milo led everyone through the front door. The place was packed with patrons.

May Randall looked up and her eyes narrowed. "Where's Twig?"

"Still in Loess," Milo replied. "Duty calls. I've more to tell you when you get a break."

May shook her head. "My waitress didn't come in this morning, so it's just me. My first break won't be 'til we're closed." She glanced around. "Have a seat once something opens up."

May went back to work, diligently taking orders and serving food. Several patrons mumbled about the service, quite unaccustomed to waiting for food in the diner. Coffee cups slid to the edge of the tables, hoping May would get the subtle hint. When a large table emptied, Milo motioned for the Brands to sit; however, Maggie didn't move. Her jaw set, she went behind the counter and picked up the coffee urn. May spotted her from the corner of her eye and—at once—a battle for the ages began.

May walked slowly toward the woman who was invading her territory.

Maggie stood her ground, unbowed.

May began to circle Maggie, who matched her step by step.

Milo watched in wonder. Two women—same age, same build, same iron resolve—stared at one another as if looking into a mirror, circling their prey like predatory cats.

Suddenly, Maggie stopped moving and her eyes softened. One word crossed her lips as an offering of peace. "Please?"

The simple request softened May's will. She answered with a simple nod.

In that instant, each of the two pioneer women grew in the eyes of the other. With a simple nod, May Randall welcomed Maggie Brand into her world, forging a bond never to be broken.

When the lunch crowd thinned, May locked the front door and flipped a wooden sign in the window from Open to Closed. She immediately went to the contributive woman and shook her hand. "Thank you for the help. I'm May Randall, this here's my place."

"I'm Maggie Brand," she said through a smile. "We're just passing through. We stopped in to see Milo. This here's my husband, Newt, my son Jacob, and his wife, Sara."

May greeted each of the Brands with a warm smile and a hearty handshake. When introductions concluded, she began wiping down the countertops as she talked. "Are you folks from Vermont?"

Without a word, Newt Brand grabbed a broom and began to sweep the floor.

Maggie's smile widened. "No, Milo helped us out of a spot of trouble down Colorado way."

"Handsome Hal Hampton?" May asked.

"He was an evil man," Sara squeezed Jacob's hand. "I'm glad he's dead."

"It's your right to be," Maggie said. She addressed May. "He tried to kill our Sara."

May glanced from Maggie to Milo. "Milo killed him instead?"

The big deputy shook his head. "Maggie and I killed him instead."

May's eyes went from Milo back to Maggie, where they stayed. "You killed him?"

"He tried killing Newt, then me," Maggie replied. "Once he started trying to kill my kin I'd had enough."

The two women stared at each other for a moment, then both smiled.

"Then, I'm glad he's dead, as well," May said. Her voice lowered. "He tried to kill you?"

"The fool rode onto my ranch one day and demanded I cater to his every whim." Maggie smiled. "I don't cotton to being bossed about, and Hampton didn't cotton to the whoopin' I gave him."

May laughed and the others joined in.

"A few days later," Maggie went on. "He kidnapped Sara and ran me down with a horse."

The backs of May's ears reddened. "Now I'm particularly happy he's dead."

Unfamiliar with parts of the story, Newt listened closely—only to be startled by May's attention. "He tried killing you as well, Mister Brand?"

"Yes, ma'am," Newt replied. "He'd have succeeded if not for Milo here."

May glanced at the big marshal. "I sense a common theme here."

"I just picked him up and dusted him off," Milo chuckled. "Wasn't much saving going on."

"He's being humble." The faintest hint of a tear gathered in Maggie's eyes. "Milo gave me back my Newt. I could never thank him enough."

Newt straightened his shoulders and looked May Randall in the eye. "There's things a man don't talk about in mixed company." He paused to gather his thoughts. "But sometimes they need to be said no matter. Milo saved my life twice; once from the buzzards, once from the bottle. I'm in debt over my head to the man."

Maggie placed her hand on her husband's and the room went silent.

May caught sight of the gesture from the corner of her eye. She turned to Milo. "Funny, Twig told me you'd never amount to much."

The room erupted in laughter.

The mood broken, May turned back to the Brands. "What are your plans from here?"

Maggie shrugged. "We're headed home to Virginia, but whether we reach there or not is in the wind."

"Are you staying here for a spell?" May asked.

"They're staying with me until they decide to dig in or move on," Milo replied.

May shook her head. "No, Milo, your place is meant for three or four people at the most." She turned to Newt and Maggie. "I have an empty house and a well-stocked bunkhouse. Perfect quarters for the lot of you until you decide what your next move is. Please, stay with me."

"We couldn't possibly," Maggie replied.

May slammed the door shut on further discussion. "You couldn't possibly not."

With that settled, May faced Milo. "Now, what's this about Twig?"

Milo proceeded to re-tell the sequence of events in Loess and how Twig stayed as an acting Sheriff.

May shook her head. "That man's always taking on more than he needs to."

Milo smiled. "Says the woman who runs a diner, a school, and a working ranch."

May allowed herself a grin. "Any idea how long?"

"He said a week to start. He'll figure things out from there."

The tremble on May's lip was barely discernable—to everyone but Maggie. Her face softened. "Your Twig sounds like a man of principle."

"He has grit coming out his ears," May replied with a wan smile. "Simply because the rocks in his head leave no room."

CHAPTER TWENTY-TWO

Galen Reid sat alone in the shadows of his private office atop the Irishman. The place was too noisy for serious work—the piano was directly downstairs, and the rent-by-the-hour rooms for his painted ladies were next door—but it afforded him a reasonable measure of privacy.

His mind roiled with emotions; Reid was in no mood to talk to anyone. Three things gnawed him, fraying the edges of his sanity. *Wes is gone* battled for traction against *Wes tried to murder me.* As conflicting as those two concepts were, they paled in comparison to—*I'm broke.* Reid sat in the dingy office, muttering to himself, "Everything I had was in that house."

Jeb Thompson finished his session with Reid's least expensive girl, and ambled down the hall toward the stairs. On an impulse, he knocked on the office door.

"Go away!"

"It's me, Jeb Thompson."

"I said go away!"

"I have business to discuss."

Thompson waited for nearly a minute before Reid responded. "Come in then."

Thompson stepped inside the musty room and spotted Reid in the corner. "Afternoon, Galen."

"What business could you possibly have with me?"

"Haven't seen you around. I was wondering if you've met the acting sheriff."

Reid's jaw tightened. "Can't say I have. What's it to you?"

"I thought you called the shots around here."

"Some say."

"I figured I was next in line for the top spot."

Reid's jowls began to jiggle and he broke into a chuckle. "You? Sheriff? Never crossed my mind."

Thompson tensed; fighting hard to curb his anger.

Reid paid no attention. "Who is he?"

"Some fella from the Kansas Marshals."

Reid leaned forward, exposing the angry red blotches on his face from his burns. "Not that one-armed bastard, is it?"

"No, some stick-thin fella. Beady eyes and a smart mouth. Issuing orders like he owns the place."

"I own Loess," Reid shot back.

"That's what I've been led to believe. But I guarantee this fella ain't gonna take orders from you."

"And you will?"

"As sheriff, I'd be your employee—I'd have to listen."

"You never did for Alf." Reid smirked and waved Thompson away.

The deputy ignored him. "Shame about Wes."

"I said leave!"

"You miss him?"

Reid said nothing. Thompson closed the door and latched the lock.

"I said leave!"

"I asked you a question. Do you miss Wes?"

"I want to kill him; I want to piss on his grave…"

Thompson was surprised when the fat man's shoulders began to heave.

"Most of all," Reid blubbered, "I want to hug him again. I—miss—him—so—much." He collapsed into a fit of sobs. "He was my only family."

Thinking the tears fanciful, Thompson raised his hand to cover a grin. After Reid regained some control, the deputy pulled up a chair.

"What if I told you…"

CHAPTER TWENTY-THREE

When Milo made it back to the Armory, he found Silas Petit scratching out paperwork with a worn-down pencil. Silas looked up when his young deputy knocked at his door, his face covered in a tired grin.

Silas rubbed his weary eyes. "Welcome back. Everything work out down there?"

Milo proceeded to relay the circumstances surrounding the investigation of the mistaken hanging of the false Hal Hampton, and the fire at Galen Reid's house. The veteran lawman laughed when told of the escape and resurrection of the ghost that was Andy Steele, yet his face tightened when told of the death of Alf Lemure.

"Sad thing," Silas shook his head. "Alf was a good lawman. I've known him since he took the Loess job five years back. He'll be missed." After a pause, he asked. "Who's filling in for him?"

"Twig."

"No better man for the job." Silas sat forward. "He'll help them find someone capable."

Milo crossed his arms. "The fool's going on about making the move permanent."

Silas' ears perked. "What gave you that impression?"

"He told me so himself."

"Was he drunk?"

"No," Milo chuckled. "Neither was I."

Silas yawned. "Twig's like a brother to me. I'd hate to lose him."

Milo put his hand on the desk and leaned in. "Then stop him."

Silas cupped his hands behind his head and took in the concern on Milo's face. His eyes softened. "I'd no more stop a man from seeking happiness than I'd stop a bear from hibernating. Both are carrying out their inbred nature."

Milo recoiled. "You'd up and let him go?"

"If it was his choice to do so."

Milo shook his head, unable to find the words to go on.

"Listen, Milo, I don't want to lose Twig. That's a given. But never lose sight of the fact that I also want no strings when I decide to move on."

Exasperated, Milo couldn't bite back his words this time around. "This change business just isn't fair."

Silas sat forward, placed his hands on the desk and stood eye-to-eye with his deputy. "Fair? The sooner you surrender that notion the better. Twig was here before I arrived, and he's done his job at a pace no one could match. If he wants to slow it down, so be it. No one deserves peace and quiet more than Twig and May Randall."

"I know all that." Milo removed his hand from the desk, his shoulders slumped. "It just doesn't make things any easier."

"Easy?" Silas barked. "The sooner you surrender that notion the better, as well."

"Understood." Despite his boss's tone, Milo smiled. "But he isn't in for anything easy in Loess just yet. He's laying naked in a pit of angry rattlesnakes."

"Even with Harms dead?"

"Even."

"Well, like I said, there's no one better. But, just in case, keep Boots fed and watered and your bedroll close at hand."

CHAPTER TWENTY-FOUR

Twig Randall sat in Sturgis Rathbone's office, deep in a conversation about appointing a new sheriff for Loess, when Galen Reid burst through the door.

"Ever heard of knocking?" Twig asked.

"And, just who are you to speak to me as such?" Reid shot back.

"The name's Twig Randall."

Reid put his hands on his hips. "I'm to assume you're the acting sheriff?"

"He's running down a list of fellas, trying to get me to recommend someone," Sturgis said.

"And?"

"And I'm doing my level best to talk him into taking the job."

"You know that's my decision to make, Sturgis."

"Why's that?" Twig asked.

"Because I own the town," Reid replied. "And I want Jeb Thompson."

The Judge shook his head. "Jeb's no more a candidate than Tommy LeBeouf."

"That's silly, Sturgis. Tom LeBeouf is the town drunk."

"Exactly."

Reid's jowls shook from anger. "May I speak with you in private, *Your Honor?*"

"No. Whatever you have to say, say it to the both of us."

Reid slammed the butt of his new walking-stick against the floor.

Sturgis glared at him. "I'll not be bullied, Galen. I'm the appointed magistrate of this town and I choose the sheriff—not you."

"You'll hear from me again!" Reid spun on his chubby heels and stormed out the door.

Twig watched him go. "Quite the fella."

"He's trouble; won't give up that easily."

"How about Jeb Thompson?"

"He's young and full of himself. He never listened to Alf, always gallivanting around without a responsibility in the world. He's harmless, unless Reid has him on the payroll. Then—well, then he'd be a force to reckon with. Good with a gun and hot tempered."

Twig leaned back in his chair. "Kansas City is full to the brim with men of that ilk. We'll deal with him down the line."

"That mean you want the job?" Sturgis grinned.

Twig shrugged. "You must eat a lot of flies with your mouth open all the time."

CHAPTER TWENTY-FIVE

On the Brand's third day in Kansas City, May Randall stopped by the Marshal's office to invite Milo to dinner. "Smokey Meeks is in town and he's making his famous roast of beef. Be there at six."

"How could I say no?"

When Milo arrived at the Randall place, he saw Newt and Jacob repairing an axle on one of their wagons. Sara sat on the porch, knitting and singing an unknown tune. May stepped onto the porch and rang the dinner bell when Milo rode into the yard.

"Wash up, food's ready!"

Milo went into the bunkhouse and scrubbed his face in the sink. When he entered the kitchen, he saw a familiar face. "Hey, Smokey."

Smokey Meeks removed a steaming cut of beef from the oven. "Howdy, Milo. I made extra since I knew you were coming."

"Enjoying the company?"

Smokey nodded. "They're fine people, Milo. Newt's a solid man, and Maggie—well, she could be May's twin."

"That's high praise coming from you," Milo said. "I know how you feel about May."

"She's like the big sister I never had," Smokey replied. "Go sit down, let's eat."

When the food was put on the table and began disappearing down various gullets, Milo heard a whimper near his foot. He glanced down at two chubby puppies. "Well, I was wondering when we'd cross paths. It's obvious Ma's been feeding you well."

"Not me, Smokey."

"Guilty as charged," the cook grinned.

"Made themselves at home, huh?"

May gave a curt nod. "You aren't getting Abbey back. I've claimed her as my own."

"Abbey, huh?" Milo scooped up the puppy. "You gonna like it here?"

She licked his nose.

"That makes it official. She's yours. But Pete goes home with me."

"Pete, huh?" Smokey asked. "I was calling him Walt."

"I always wanted a friend named Pete." Milo scooped up the male. "Looks like a Pete to me, so Pete it is."

When dinner concluded, the group moved into the living room for conversation. The Brands told of their trip east and Milo related the story of Andy Steele and the mess in Loess.

When Milo finished, May addressed Smokey. "Do you think you could handle things around here for a time?"

The cook shrugged. "Sure."

May turned to Milo. "It's not in my nature to ask, but can you ride with me to Loess? I miss my Twig something fierce."

Milo scratched Pete behind the ears. "Of course."

"I'll ride along if it's all right with you," Newt chimed in. "I'd like to stretch my legs."

"May goes, we all go," Maggie declared.

****

157

The next morning, Milo arrived at the Randall place before the sun. The wagons were loaded and the teams hitched. At first light, everyone took their places, said so long to Smokey, and started south. May Randall fell in step with Milo, their horses out in front, moving slowly to keep pace with the wagons. Pete and Abbey had places of honor on the front seat next to Maggie.

After a short time, May addressed her riding partner. "Those are some mighty fine folks, Milo. Maggie told me what happened in Monroe. I'm glad you were there to help."

"All part of the job."

"You sound like Twig."

Milo's tone grew serious. "He was worried about you when we rode for Loess."

"He worries if I stub my toe. He's a good man."

"It ain't every day you kill a man, Ma."

May's face softened. "Thank goodness."

"He's worried Kansas City's getting too dangerous."

"I share the same worry for him." She glanced at the lawman. "And for you."

"Twig's good with a gun. He'll be fine."

"You know what he always says, no matter how fast you are, there's always someone faster."

CHAPTER TWENTY-SIX

Still in the dark as to why he was summoned, Shanks Morris knocked lightly on the front door of Jeb Thompson's shanty. Thompson called out for him to enter, and Shanks pushed through the poorly-hung door. He gagged at the stench, but found his fellow deputy pouring a glass of whiskey in the far corner.

"What'd you want from me, Jeb?"

"Come all the way in, Shanks. I poured you a glass."

Shanks moved into the light of the window and accepted the half-full glass. Thompson stepped aside, and Wes Harms came into view, twirling his black derby.

Shanks nearly dropped his glass. "They said you were dead."

"Far as they know, I still am."

"What do the two of you want with me?"

Harms sneered and ran his finger along the hawk feather of his hat. "Jeb and I are going to take over Loess. We want you to join us."

"What of Galen?"

"What of him?" Wes replied. "He either steps aside or we bury him."

Shanks took a step back, running full on into the wall. "The new sheriff?'

"I'm gonna kill him," Thompson growled.

Shanks' eyes widened. "But, he's a good fella."

"He's a dead man," Harms said as he drew his weapon.

Thompson flinched, but said nothing.

Harms went on, his voice menacing. "You in or out, Shanks?"

"I want no part in any killing." Shanks put his hands out in front of him.

"The only killing today will be yours." Harms shot him in the chest.

Shanks fell forward. Thompson caught him midair, eased him to the ground, checking for a pulse. "He's dead. You killed him. He..."

160

Harms shifted his barrel to cover the big deputy.

"He didn't need to die," Thompson stammered. "Shanks was my friend. He'd have left town if we'd have told him to."

"He'd have made it as far as the sheriff's office, where he'd have blown our whole plan." Harms cocked his trigger. "There's no turning back now. Are you all the way in, or are you out?"

Thompson stared at the still-smoking gun and swallowed. "All the way in."

CHAPTER TWENTY-SEVEN

Never one to remain idle when either money or power was involved, Galen Reid sat in his hastily thrown together office atop the Irishman, speaking heatedly with a short, muscular man.

"I tell you, Sam, this acting sheriff is a menace."

"Folks I've spoken to say he's a reasonable fella."

"Jeb Thompson is twice the man!"

Sam McLaren had heard enough. "Size-wise maybe, but Jeb ain't got enough brains to take a bath once a month, let alone run a town as head lawman."

"But, he's…"

"He's an idiot, Galen. You only want him in charge so you can tell him when and where to do your bidding."

"But, Alf…"

"Alf Lemure was a good man—had a backbone—and you didn't cotton to his independence. You see an opportunity to put someone in charge who ain't got a lick of sense. Folks'll get hurt and it'll be bad for the future of Loess." McLaren rose to leave. "I want nothing to do with this lunacy."

Reid put up his piggish hands to stop him. "Here me out, Sam. We're in line to hit it big here."

"If you want Loess to grow, folks'll have to feel comfortable working and living here. Bad men like Johnny McAlister and Wes Harms didn't allow for such comfort."

"You bite your tongue. McAlister was who he was, but Wes was a good boy."

"Wes bullied the businesses in this town and terrorized its citizens. I can't say I'm sorry he's gone."

"I should beat you senseless for saying that."

McLaren bowed his neck. "Give it a go."

Reid cowed, using the only weapon at his disposal—the power of money. He stood, his jowls quivering. "I own this damned town, Sam. You work for me, so you'll do as I say."

Despite Reid's bulk, McLaren easily pushed past him. "I work for you, but I don't answer to you."

Although it was just past noon, Sam McLaren stomped down the back steps of the Irishman, intending to soak his anger in a bottle of whiskey downstairs. Suddenly he stopped in his tracks and detoured across the street, straight to Sturgis Rathbone's office. He was still hot under the collar when he knocked three times and was summoned inside.

"Sam, pleasure to see you this time of day," Sturgis said. "Shouldn't you be at your store?"

"I was summoned for a meeting," Sam replied. "Turned out to be a waste of effort."

"Well, come in," Sturgis replied. "There's someone I'd like you to meet who is definitely worth your valuable time."

A thin gentleman with steely eyes stood from his chair.

"Twig Randall, this here's Sam McLaren, the de facto mayor of this town."

"Greetings, Mister Mayor," Twig said.

Sam's anger fizzled at the misunderstanding. "I've never actually been voted or appointed to the post, but..."

"But he runs the place," Sturgis interrupted. "Reid owns it, Sam makes it work."

Twig's eyes narrowed at the mention of Reid's name.

164

Sam noticed. "You got your bearings on Galen Reid yet, Mister Randall?"

"It ain't my custom to speak poorly of others."

"Even if they deserve it," Sturgis added.

"Well, I've no such moral code," Sam said. "This place could be a paradise if it weren't for the meddling fingers of Galen Reid. He might have built the skeleton of Loess, but he hasn't the personal wherewithal to provide it with a brain or a heart."

Twig chewed on the words for a moment. "So, there's more than meets the eye there?"

Sam shook his head. "When it comes to Reid, there's less than meets the eye."

Sturgis offered Sam a chair, but the businessman waved it off. "I just stopped in to say howdy. I've got an appointment with a bottle of whiskey."

Twig extended his hand. "It was a pleasure making your company, Sam."

"I'm not prone to shenanigans, Mister Randall, so I'm going to spill my guts. I just came from Reid's office wherein he attempted to besmirch you to curry favor with the idea of appointing Jeb Thompson as permanent Sheriff in these parts."

165

"That's what we were just discussing," Sturgis responded.

"I think it's a poor excuse of a grab for power," Sam snapped. "Might as well put a hat and badge on a wild boar. We'd probably be better off."

Sturgis laughed, while Twig studied the face of Sam McLaren.

"Did he mention any plans on running me off?" Twig asked.

"Nothing specific, but, if I were you, I'd keep my eyes peeled, Mister Randall." Sam shook his head. "Galen Reid is a bully and Jeb Thompson is his cudgel."

CHAPTER TWENTY-EIGHT

As Sam McLaren whisked out, the two sides of the door flapped back and forth like the wings of a bird. Before they'd settled, a familiar face stepped inside unannounced.

"Milo!" Twig shouted. "What in tarnation?"

"Come on outside, you two. There's someone here to see you."

Twig stepped onto the raised boardwalk, his eyes darting about. When they settled on his wife, he bolted for the warmth of her arms. When the excitement of the reunion began to ebb, introductions were made and accommodations mapped out. Andy came out to help carry luggage and Maggie pointed directly at him. "You! I thought you were dead!"

"It's all right, Maggie," Milo chuckled. "This here's Andy Steele from Texas. He's riding with me."

"Spitting image," she mumbled.

Milo glanced over his shoulder at Andy. "See why they hung you down in Loess?"

Andy's hand reflexively rubbed his neck.

Sara let out a whimper. Jacob whisked forward and took his wife's hand. "The resemblance has sent me to a dark place."

"To Handsome Hal Hampton?" May asked.

"Yes, I said it before he was an evil man," Sara chimed in. "And, he wasn't handsome."

Milo laughed aloud. "Sorry, Andy."

Sara blushed, while Andy joined Milo's laughter.

"Andy here's a young man with quite a story to tell," Milo responded. "Let's have him tell it over lunch. I'm starved."

After the meal, Andy went back to the sheriff's office, while Twig pulled Milo aside. Milo dragged Newt along.

"There might be trouble brewin' down here." Twig glanced between Milo and Newt.

"Speak freely," Milo said. "Newt has my confidence."

"All right," Twig went on, "it seems Galen Reid is out for my hide. Wants to replace me with Jeb Thompson."

"I don't know much about Jeb," Milo replied, "except for the fact he wasn't around the night Alf was killed."

"He was drunk, down at the bordello."

"To use your logic," Milo said, "let's figure our pluses and minuses. We know Reid and Thompson are against you, but is there anyone you can count on?"

"Sturgis. Maybe Rod Newby. Andy, but he's raw."

"The Mute's a good man," Milo said. "He's a plus. How about Shanks Morris?"

"I haven't seen much of him. Thompson told me Shanks has a case of the piles and can't sit a horse."

In spite of himself, Newt laughed. Milo and Twig joined in shortly.

"There's another man I can count on," Twig said. "Local fella by the name of McLaren. Town's mayor. That said, Reid's got all the money in these parts, and lots of folks beholden to him. Hard to say if Thompson can wrangle a mess of 'em together into a rag-tag gang."

Milo rubbed the stump of his missing left hand. "I was planning on starting back right away. You want me to stick around 'til this festers to a head?"

Newt Brand cut in. "He's got my gun, and he can count Jacob, as well."

Twig nodded to the stranger. "No use you getting tangled up in this, Mister Brand."

Newt motioned over his shoulder, drawing Twig's attention to two women engaged in a joyful conversation over two wrestling puppies. "You've missed a few things while you were gone. Your wife met her spiritual selfsame a few days back." Newt chuckled. "Mister Randall, I get the feeling we'll never get those two apart ever again. We ain't going nowhere until you do. Count us among your pluses."

While the men talked, Jacob and Sara took the puppies and wandered off to acquaint themselves with the town. Free to do as they pleased, Maggie and May stepped into McLaren's Dry Goods for supplies. Preoccupied with each other, neither noticed when a tall man with greasy hair followed them inside. The two women began to talk as they picked out essentials, laughter following them through the aisles. That stopped when the man stepped in their way, leering as he approached.

"Mind if I ask just who you ladies are?"

Maggie fixed him with a stare. "What's it to you?"

The man's face went from a leer to a menace. "I'm the law around here."

"That's a curiosity," Maggie shot back. "Seems as though her husband's the acting sheriff."

May Randall stood firm, her shoulders back.

The tall man grabbed a heavy jar of pole beans off the shelf, leaned forward, and dropped them into May Randall's purse.

"Well, then," he sneered. "He'll be the first one we talk to about your thievery from the longstandin' townsfolk."

May drew the beans from her purse and stiffened. "I haven't stolen anything."

"I say you have—saw it with my own eyes." The man leaned forward, bullying them with his size. "And what I say's all that matters."

Maggie didn't budge. "You're a liar."

"Out here, a man's word'll always outweigh a woman's."

"She's not one woman," Maggie cut in. "There's a pair of us."

"That's of nevermind." The goon reached out and grabbed May by the arm. "Come along peaceful now."

May struggled against him, but his grip was strong.

"Let go of her," Maggie shouted. She turned and grabbed a cast iron skillet off a shelf, bringing it down hard across the brute's wrist.

The brute screamed out in pain.

May reacted in an instant, hitting him square in the crotch with the jar of beans. The big man threw her aside and she crashed into a shelf of flour. He immediately wrapped his hands around Maggie's neck and began to squeeze. May recovered and swung the heavy glass jar. It slammed against the side of his face, knocking him to the ground. In a rage, he leapt to his feet—only to be stopped in his tracks by the business end of a double-barreled shotgun.

"Steady where you are, Jeb, or I'll unleash a fury on you."

"The lady's stealing from you, Sam," Jeb Thompson glowered.

Sam's voice was calm, but stern. "No, she isn't. I saw what you did with *my* own eyes." He looked back and forth between the two women. "What do you ladies want me to do with the scoundrel?"

"No harm done in the short-term." May squared on the crimson-faced deputy. "As for the long-term, I will be discussing this with my husband."

Sam lowered the shotgun and waived Thompson away. Expecting an outburst toward the women, Sam was surprised when Thompson's anger focused on him.

"I can't believe you sided with out-of-towners, Sam. You'll pay for this."

McLaren glanced around at the broken shelf and scattered merchandise. "And you'll pay for all this. I'll see to it."

Thompson shouldered past the grocer and rumbled out the front door. Sam took up a broom and started cleaning up. "You ladies all right?"

"Who was that man?" May asked.

"His name's Jeb Thompson."

"Is he the actual law around here, as he says?" Maggie asked.

"He'd like to be," Sam answered. "He's more a part of the problem than anything else."

Maggie grabbed the broom from him and started to sweep, her pace as furious as her mood.

May started to work on the shelf, her deft hands piecing it back together. "The nerve of the man! We haven't even been here an hour and we've already made an enemy."

"Did I hear you say you're Sheriff Randall's wife?" Sam asked.

May's eyes never strayed from her task. "You did."

"Then Jeb was your enemy long before you came across the town limits. Keep your eyes open. Jeb Thompson's a fool."

"We will." May finished with the shelf and faced Sam. "Twig's calling himself Sheriff Randall already?"

Sam shrugged his shoulders. "No, ma'am, just wishful thinking on my part." A customer entered the store with a question to ask. Sam turned for the register. "You ladies pick out what you need, it's on me."

As the two women were finishing their shopping, a young couple strolled down the boardwalk, pausing to look into the store windows. Two small puppies, tethered by thin ropes, walked in front of them, barking and wagging their tails at the passing patrons. When they paused in front of the Irishman, a heavy-set man in a tailored suit pushed out of the swinging double doors, nearly stepping on Pete Thorne's fuzzy head.

Galen Reid froze, without an apology, eyeing the intruding dogs. His gaze then switched to the couple, scanning their appearance for acceptability. "I don't believe I've made your acquaintance." His tone dripped of haut.

"Our names are Jacob and Sara Brand. We're newly arrived from Monroe, Colorado."

"Never heard of it," Reid shot back. "What brings you here?"

"Just visiting," Sara replied. "We're friends with the sheriff."

Reid's eyes narrowed. "Loess recently lost its sheriff; therefore, we are currently without. About whom do you speak?"

Confused, Jacob mumbled, "Sheriff Randall?"

Reid's face tomatoed. "The cretin's calling himself Sheriff Randall now?"

"That's how we were introduced," Sara replied. "We just met…"

Reid didn't wait for her to finish. "Truth be told, we are currently being lorded over by an unwelcome member of the Kansas Marshals."

Startled, the Brands didn't answer.

Reid's upper lip curled. "I wouldn't expect young folks like yourself to understand such things."

Sara's back bowed. "I'm old enough to recognize boorishness."

Unaccustomed to her tone, Reid leaned in. "Now, see here, young lady, I own this town. You shouldn't address a man of my stature in such a manner."

"I have spent about as much time with you as I have with Sheriff Randall," Sara replied. "And I can assure you, he inspires respect, while you arrogantly demand it. Maybe it is you who lacks understanding."

Reid raised his hand.

Jacob stepped between them. "You lay as much as a finger on my wife and you'd better own a cemetery, as well."

Reid's jowls trembled, yet he lowered his hand. "See to it that you mind your manners in Loess. While you might be on good terms with the so-called acting sheriff, I retain domain over this town, and I'm not a man to cross." Reid glanced between the pair, then lowered his eyes to Pete and Abbey. "And keep those mongrels off our boardwalk, or I'll have them banned forthwith."

When they reached the street, Maggie and May found Twig and Milo still deep in conversation. Twig took one look at his wife and his face hardened. "What's the matter?"

176

"There's a pebble in our shoe already," May said.

Twig's eyebrows furrowed. "How so?"

May relayed the story of the encounter with Jeb Thompson. Twig's back stiffening with every word.

"Go on about your business," he growled. "I'll handle this."

"We'll handle this," Milo added.

"No, Milo, this is my jurisdiction—my fight."

Milo shook his head. "Seems to me *we* are both sworn marshals of the State of Kansas. Last time I heard, Loess was smack dab on the Kansas map. This is *our* fight."

Resigned to the fact, Twig nodded. "So be it."

"Where's Newt," Maggie asked.

"He went to the livery about your wagon," Milo answered.

"You want me to fetch him?" she asked.

Twig shook his head. "No, ma'am. You folks stay out of this. Let's keep you under a cloud of peace until the thunder starts."

Twig marched down the middle of the street with Milo in tow. When they ducked into the Broken Shoe, Spike Duggan stepped out from behind the bar to meet them.

"Thompson," Twig grunted.

The big bartender pointed up the stairs. "Last door on the right." As the two lawmen started to climb, Duggan grabbed his blackjack. "You want some help?"

Milo waved him off. "Unless you see both of us at the base of the stairs in a heap—thanks, but no thanks."

When they reached the door, they didn't bother to knock. Twig turned the handle and slammed it open. Sensing danger, Trixie broke the octopus grip of Jeb Thompson and swept past the lawmen.

"What the hell do you want, runt?" Thompson bellowed as he leapt from the bed.

"A piece of your hide," Twig shot back.

"For what cause?"

"How dare you lay a hand on my wife," Twig roared. "Especially in the name of the law."

Thompson scowled at him. "You ain't nothin' without that big fella behind you."

Twig turned to Milo. "You stay out of this."

Thompson lowered his head and rushed the smaller man, but Twig was faster. His hands flashed, raining down punches on the ogreish tough. Thompson roared with each blow, trying to dodge, but each movement placed him in line another with perfectly delivered fist. Seeing no options, Thompson again tried to bully Twig with his size, but the smaller man used his quickness—kicking and punching with the fervor of pent up anger.

Before long, Thompson raised his hands over his battered face and surrendered. "Enough."

Twig stepped back; his hands covered in Thompson's blood. "Get out of town and don't come back. Next time we skirmish, fists won't be my weapon of choice."

As the two made their way back through town, Twig stopped Milo. "I hate to ask again, but as a favor to me, hustle back to Kansas City and let Silas know what's going on down here. Tell him I don't know when I'll be return on account I'm up to my ankles in alligators."

Despite the events of the past hour, Milo saw a happiness in Twig that hadn't been there since the incident at May's Diner. "You sure you don't want me to stay?"

"I've handled a hundred men tougher than Jeb Thompson. I'll be fine."

"All right then, I'll get my gear ready and say my goodbyes."

The two men shook hands.

"Oh, and Milo," Twig hesitated. "Thanks for bringing Ma down. I sure missed her."

"She had the same sentiments," Milo chuckled. "Now, I've got a bit of advice for you."

Twig's eyebrows raised.

"Give Newt a chance to crack that shell of yours. He and Jacob are good men. Plus, he's right—Ma and Maggie are joined at the hip." Milo smiled. "Damn, I'm glad they're on our side."

Twig started for the office, while Milo sauntered for the livery. As he neared the corner, Milo glanced over his shoulder. Twig stood watching him go—still as a statue.

He's never coming back, Milo thought to himself. *He's found himself a new home.*

****

A hundred feet away, a battered Jeb Thompson ushered Wes Harms through the back door of the Broken Shoe and quietly up the stairs. The two padded unseen down the hall—by everyone but Spike Duggan, who was retrieving a bottle of rotgut whiskey from the storeroom. When the pair reached the last door on the upstairs hallway, Thompson knocked softly. A

180

pair of delicate hands open the door from inside—the hands of Galen Reid.

Reid burst into tears upon seeing his resurrected nephew. He beckoned Harms into a hug, and he reluctantly agreed. After a brief moment, Reid pushed Harms to arms-length—and slapped him full-force across his right cheek.

"You stupid—" Reid yelled.

Harms reached for the fat man's neck with outstretched fingers. "You son-of-a—"

Thompson tackled Harms and the two men tumbled over the bed onto the wood floor.

"Remember why we're here, Wes!"

Harms relaxed in the ex-deputy's grip. Thompson helped him to his feet, where he picked up his derby and straightened the singed hawk feather. Uncle and nephew glared at each other. All were startled at a sharp rap on the door.

The gruff voice of the big bartender filled the room. "You all right in there, Boss?"

Reid straightened his lapels. "I'm fine, Spike."

Reid waited for the footsteps to retreat before he spoke. "He'll be back, if I need him."

Harms pulled back his jacket, revealing a holstered pistol. "And I'll kill him."

"Like you tried to kill me?"

"You pushed me too far, Uncle Galen."

"Can't you both forget that?" Thompson broke in. "And let's get on with business at hand?"

"Forget that he tried to kill me, and in the process destroyed everything I own?"

"I thought you said he'd play along, Wes."

"Play along with what?"

"We're going to take back Loess," Harms scowled. "With, or without, your help."

"I do lament that outsiders are taking over my town. But, the Randall fella has too much behind him. Newby, Shanks…"

"Not Shanks," Harms replied in a casual tone.

"He's loyal to the badge," Reid said.

"Was," Harms chuckled. "He was the first casualty in our little war."

"Shanks was a good man."

"Like I said—was." Harms chuckled again. "He wanted out, how about you?"

"Wes, this is madness." Reid took a step back, his face paled, with the exception of the new burn scars.

Harms glowered at him. "Who you calling mad? I tried to kill you once, I won't fail the second time."

Reid flinched.

Thompson tried to get them back on track. "Tell him the plan."

For the first time since he'd entered the room, Reid focused on the deputy. "What happened to your face?"

"Randall."

"That little fella did that to you?"

"He had help," Thompson lied. "The one-handed marshal."

"A one-handed man and that willow-wisp sheriff did that to you?'

"The little man has grit." Thompson growled as he balled his fists.

"Save it for them," Harms said. "They'll get theirs."

"The Thorne fella is back in town?" Reid asked. "What does that do to the plans?"

"That big lummox is dumb as a rock," Harms blustered. "He'll be no problem. Leave him to me." Harms then laid out the steps they were to take for revenge on the outsiders. Reid listened intently, his interest going from abject horror to gradual acceptance.

"This will work, Uncle Galen. It has to. I want Loess free from the outsiders." Harms took a deep, gulping breath. "I want things back to normal."

Reid rubbed his numerous chins. "It *might* work, with some measure of luck. And, I agree, I'd sure like it if things returned to normal. The interlopers are multiplying. I met two of their ungainly offspring today. But, Wes, there's big risk here—kidnapping's a hanging offense."

"And murder isn't?" Harms snickered. "I'm in up to my hips already, so I might as well go in over my head."

"What if the Kansas Marshals find out? They bring far greater resources."

"Then I'll kill as many of them as I can," Harms hissed. "Especially that one-handed bastard." He calmed himself. "All you have to do, Uncle Galen, is get that Randall fella alone."

"For what meager gain?"

"Meager or not, we're taking back what's ours."

"But it's not yours," Reid spluttered. "It's mine."

This time Harms answered with a throaty laugh. "Was."

CHAPTER TWENTY-NINE

That night, May and Twig Randall settled into the cozy confines of Sturgis Rathbone's guest house. Needing more room, the Brand family set up inside the modest residence vacated by the death of Alf Lemure. Twig and May nuzzled on the couch, while Abbey played with a sock monkey made especially for her.

"I think you'll like it down here, Ma," Twig said.

"Permanently or as a vacation?"

"At least 'til they pick a new sheriff. Maybe a month or so, he sighed. "Beyond that, you never can tell."

"What's got you sold on Loess?"

"A solitude that Kansas City lacks."

"Sounds like there's folks down here who aren't on the up and up."

"There's a few bugs at the picnic," Twig grinned, "but they ain't into the tater salad yet."

"You and your metaphors."

"I don't know what a metaphor is. I just know Loess ain't a burlap sack full of tomcats like Kansas City." He looked his wife in the eye. "That shooting at the diner's got me ruffled."

"Me too," May admitted.

"Maybe a few days away'll give us time to think about things. All's well at home?"

"Smokey's got things under control."

****

The Brands sat around Alf's dining room table, talking of the future and making plans.

"I'm glad we got away from the big city," Maggie said. "Can't see how folks could live so crowded."

"A man couldn't spit without hitting someone," Jacob added. "The place gave me the shakes."

"It's nice here," Newt said. "More like Monroe. Folks I've met seemed friendly."

"No one knows me here," Sara said. "That gives me some comfort."

"You're a married woman now," Maggie replied. "That's all anyone needs to know."

"We met a man earlier today who sassed us something fierce," Jacob said. "Said he owned the town, wasn't at all happy to see us."

"Heavy-set man?" Newt asked.

"Yes, sir."

"The man's name is Reid. Twig told me he's encountered resistance from him."

"From what I see, I wouldn't fret. Mister Randall is quite capable." Maggie stretched her arms and shook her shoulders. "All the riding in a wagon's got me bushed."

"Me too," Newt replied.

"How long you think we'll stay before we push east?" Sara asked.

Maggie shrugged. "Hard to say. Could be tomorrow, could be a month. Why do you ask?"

Sara glanced at Jacob, who smiled, then nodded. "Tell her," he whispered.

"Tell me what?" Maggie asked.

"Go or stay, either is fine by me," Sara smiled. "But we'd better hurry—I'm with child."

****

"Maggie seems like a nice woman," Twig said. "I hear tell you've grown close."

May sat up. "You heard right. She's good people—all the Brands are. But, that Maggie, well, I've never met her equal. Solid stock, skin to bone. There's times I wonder if she isn't a long-lost sister I crossed paths with on fate's account."

"Strong sentiments."

"Warranted. She ran her own ranch over in Colorado. Raised prize beef." May paused for a breath and went on. "She told me the story of how…"

Twig watched her as she talked. Her face was animated and her voice registered an excitement not heard since they'd first met. The change was both subtle and drastic in equal measure. Whatever it was, Twig welcomed it in place of the doldrums she'd suffered after the diner incident.

She's smiling again.

****

When the kerfuffle died down, Jacob and Sara excused themselves for bed, as holding in a secret of such consequence proved exhausting. Maggie and Newt sat on the sofa, warming their newly rekindled romance by the fire.

"Oh, Newt, isn't it exciting—a baby. Never thought I'd see the day."

She nearly fainted when her husband dried a tear.

"It's a dream come true," he said with a cracked voice.

Without thinking, she offered him her handkerchief. Instinctively, he accepted it and wiped his cheeks. Maggie took him in as she never had. His face newly scarred, his hair speckled gray. His eyes, those steely eyes, held emotion she'd never known he was capable of. The change was both subtle and drastic in equal measure. Whatever it was, she welcomed it after having lost him to the bottom of a whiskey bottle for so long.

He's feeling again.

CHAPTER THIRTY

A week passed quietly in Loess—too quiet by Twig's reasoning—yet his mind warmed to the slower pace. His daily work routine consisted of carrying out the orders issued by Judge Rathbone, while avoiding those of Galen Reid. The lull of work afforded the luxury of roaming his jurisdiction— meeting the ranchers and hearing their concerns—all the while secretly scouting the land. Dinner with the Brands became a nightly occurrence. From that familiarity grew a burgeoning friendship with Newt Brand, who became Twig's frequent companion on his forays around the countryside. Twig's newfound love of Loess paled to that of Newt, who surveyed the possibilities of the area with a knowing eye. The former rancher was taken by the fertile soil and abundant water supply. Both men came to a firm agreement on the town's bright future.

One plot of land caught Newt's eye above all others—nestled between the foothills and the river on the edge of town. "This here's the place I covet," Newt said as the two skirted the trail along the slow-moving water. "Far enough from town to provide sanctuary, yet not a bother to visit. A man could grow enough food to feed every man, woman, and child in Kansas."

A burned-out house and once-opulent barn signified the current owner's wealth.

"Galen Reid's place," Twig said.

"Ain't he the fella that runs the town?"

"Owns, yes. Runs, no."

"Jacob and Sara had a run-in with him the same day you *reformed* that bullish deputy's behavior."

"Reid blusters more'n his fair share, but his teeth aren't as sharp as his tongue."

"How'd his house burn?"

Twig told the story of Wes Harms, his attempt on Galen Reid's life, and the murder of Alf Lemure.

Newt's face betrayed no judgment until the demise of Twig's predecessor. "This Harms fella killed the Sheriff?"

191

"Cleaved his head with a hammer."

Newt cringed. "Not a way I'd prefer to meet the Maker."

"And, what would be the preferred method?"

"Swimmin' in a cool river on a hot day, escorted to the clouds by a bevy of angels who feed me apple pie with a scoop of fresh churned ice cream."

"Vanilla?"

"If they served apple pie with strawberry ice cream, your destination's down, not up."

The two men chuckled all the way to town. When they got there, both were surprised to see the tall, muscular form of Milo Thorne rocking in a chair outside the sheriff's office.

Twig grinned at his old partner. "I thought I told you to run along home."

"I did, but Silas reminded me that I had a few days of vacation to use and suggested fishing down at Langer's."

"The women know you're here?" Twig asked.

"Happier to see Pete than they were me."

Twig grinned, and the two men shared a glance filled with the understanding of those who'd faced danger together.

"That Silas is a right fine man," Twig sighed.

"There isn't an owl in Kansas any wiser," Milo replied.

Before the three men could retreat into the sheriff's office, Sturgis Rathbone stepped onto the boardwalk and waved them over.

"Howdy, Milo," the judge called. "I thought you'd gone home."

"Vicious rumor," Milo grinned.

"Come on in," Sturgis said. "We've something of interest to discuss."

Milo and Twig started across the street, while Newt held back.

Twig rounded on him. "Come along, Newt."

"I don't know, Twig. I..."

"Am I gonna have to drag you along?" Milo smiled.

Newt grinned back and followed. When they got inside, Twig motioned Newt forward.

"Your Honor, this here's Newt Brand, from down Colorado way. He's a friend of Milo's," Twig glanced at Newt, "and of me."

Newt shook the judge's hand.

"How'd you get mixed up with this rag-tag crew?" Sturgis asked.

Newt and Milo exchanged a quick glance.

"Milo saved my life a couple of months ago."

"Seems like these two are inclined toward that purpose," Sturgis replied.

"Newt's salt of the earth, Your Honor," Milo said. "Solid as the day is long."

Newt was surprised when he felt himself blush. "Thank you, Milo. The truth is, Judge, Milo and I crossed tracks on account of Hal Hampton. He tried killing me. He tried killing Milo. You know, the usual way folks' bond in the west."

The lawmen laughed.

"In all honesty," Newt went on. "Hampton tried killing my wife first. Rode onto the ranch and demanded she cook him a meal."

Twig's eyebrows rose at the new information.

"Is she still with us?" Sturgis asked.

"Oh, yes. She beat him silly and run him off the property," Newt chuckled. "My Maggie doesn't take kindly to being told what to do."

"I can vouch for that," Milo added.

When the laughter quieted, Twig spoke. "What'd you have for me, Judge?"

"Curious thing," Sturgis said. "I just talked to the town mortician, Zeb Jenkins. He finished sifting through the rubble of Galen Reid's barn on my orders." He paused. "There was no body found inside."

Milo processed the information in silence.

Twig slapped his hat against his leg. "Some bugs you just can't kill."

****

Supper that night was filled with shared stories and hearty laughter. Plans were made for the newly announced baby, as well as other future matters. Milo sat back and watched the two families, his heart full seeing his friends becoming friends. When the table was cleared, Milo, Twig and Newt sat in the den, digesting their meals in silence. Milo was a million miles away in thought.

"What are you smiling about," Newt asked him. "You know something we don't?"

"Just content, that's all."

"What drew you there?" Twig asked.

"At this point, all I care about is my friends being happy and safe."

"But what is it *you* want, Milo?" Twig asked.

195

Milo searched his thoughts, stumbling over the words to answer the seemingly simple question. May and Maggie entered the room and their energy drew the men away from the conversation—but not Milo from his thoughts. He left later that evening, having not muttered another word—Twig's sincere question still unanswered.

****

Across town, Rod Newby finished his drink in the Irishman, said his goodbyes, and dawdled into the street. The lone light coming from the room above the Broken Shoe faded in and out of an alcohol-fueled haze. Undaunted by the challenge of finding his way home in the tightening clutches of inebriation, he started for the corral. He'd almost made it when Jeb Thomson lassoed him and drug him into the shadows behind the bordello.

"What the—What's the meaning of this, Jeb?"

Wes Harms stepped out of the darkness. "Shut up, Mute."

Newby's eyes widened. "You're supposed to be—"

"I know, but, I ain't."

Thompson drew his gun and loosened the rope.

Newby stood free, but tense. "What do you want?"

"We're taking over Loess," Thompson said matter-of-factly. "Are you in or out?"

"What do you mean—taking over?"

"Exactly how it sounds," Harms replied. "And we're going to kill anyone in our way to get it."

"You want to be a part, Rod—yes or no?" Thompson asked.

"No." The answer was firm.

"As I figured," Thompson replied. "So, I'll give you a choice—run or die."

Harms stepped forward. "No choices. Kill him like we did Shanks and be done with it."

Newby's voice softened. "You killed Shanks, Jeb? He was your friend."

Thompson's eyes dropped.

Harms drew his weapon. "I killed him, Mute. Just like I'm gonna kill you."

"No." Thompson put his arm out, blocking Harms. "I gave him a choice."

"He'll blab his mouth, you fool."

"No, he won't. Why do you think they call him the Mute? He'll be fine." He turned to Newby. "I'll ask you again, Rod. What'll it be—run or die?"

"Not much of a choice to make, Jeb. I'd rather cow than suffer death."

"I figured you as a runner." Thompson shook his head. "Get out and don't come back. If I see you again, there'll be no second offer."

Newby started for the street, but stopped directly in front of the disgraced deputy. "Shanks was my friend too, Jeb."

"Go on, Rod. Run as far as you can."

CHAPTER THIRTY-ONE

The next day, the Randalls and the Brands met for lunch at the Irishman. Normally a jovial meal, on this occasion Twig was sullen.

As she buttered her bread, May noticed her husband's gloom. "Is the milk sour, or is it just you?"

"Something's afoot," Twig replied, his tone a bit too casual.

May passed a bowl of summer squash down the table. "How's that?"

"Rod Newby's missing. I searched for him all morning. No one's seen him."

"Is he on a bender?" Newt asked as he chewed a sandwich. "I've got some experience in that area."

"He's a drinker," Twig replied, "but he's never missed a minute of work on account of the bottle. I wouldn't even mention it, except—"

May's eyebrows raised. "Except what?"

Twig laid down his knife and scratched his ear. "Except Shank Morris has been gone quite a piece, and Jeb Thompson ain't been heard of since I run him off."

Newt took another bite. "That's all three of your deputies, ain't it?"

"Sure is." Twig put his hands on the table. "My senses tell me trouble's brewing."

May put her hand on his. "Your senses are never wrong. Where's Milo?"

"Andy and him rode out to Langer's Hole early this morning. Won't be back 'til afternoon."

"What can we do to help?" Newt asked.

Twig picked up the knife and resumed slicing. "Keep your guns loaded and your ears open. Other'n that, not much to do 'til something happens."

Maggie's brow furrowed. "What if that's too late?"

Twig forced a smile. "Put some pretty flowers o'er me and say lotsa nice words."

200

May and Maggie exchanged a furtive look, as did Twig and Newt.

"Heck, trouble's always afoot when you tote a badge," Twig chuckled. "It'll work itself out. Pass the bread, please."

****

Andy and Milo set a leisurely pace on their ride out to Langer's Hole, enjoying the warm breeze and rolling hills. As relaxing as the morning unfolded, the afternoon proved to be equally frustrating. The Hole, the epitome of an easy mark, pitched them a blank. Worms, grasshoppers, bread from their lunch—nothing drew a bite.

Milo threw his hands up. "Well, Mister Steele, seems we've run into a mystery."

"An anomaly."

"Spoken like an educated man," Milo said. "Educated or not, neither of us amounts to a fisherman. We'll likely be the first in town history to come back without scads of fish."

"That's fine on my account," Andy grinned. "I can't stand the taste of trout."

The two men shared a laugh and mounted up for the ride back. Andy started for the main trail, but Milo waved him onto a narrower path that led through the rolling foothills. In a few minutes, they topped out by an empty farmhouse on a large patch of sun-splashed fallow land. Milo called a halt and slid from his saddle.

"What's the matter, Marshal?"

"Not a thing in the world." Milo bent and ran his hand through the dirt, coming up with a large clod of dark earth. He crumbled it, sniffed the rich minerals, and examined the quality of the fertile soil, nodding as he did so.

"Beautiful piece of property. You know the owner?"

Milo grinned. "Yes, I do."

"Doesn't look like it's been worked in a while."

"About a year. But it will be this coming season."

"Owner selling the place, or something?"

"Nope," Milo chuckled. "He'll just be free to work it." He turned and pointed across the river to where a shallow, tree-lined box canyon butted up against the opposite bank. "That there's the prettiest spot in the entire State of Kansas."

A man could build him a handsome home there."

"Yes, he could," Milo sighed, his mind somewhere in a dream.

"You know the owner of that piece too?"

"I'm familiar with him," Milo smiled. His mind cleared and he swung up into his saddle. "Let's get back to town. No trout for lunch means I'm starving."

****

Just shy of three o'clock, Twig Randall sat at his desk, writing out the facts and clues of his missing deputy situation. He glanced up when Galen Reid waddled into the office.

"You have to come, Sheriff. A man's been injured out where they're working on my new barn. He's hurt bad."

"Did you get the doctor?"

"That's my next stop," Reid spluttered. "I figured you'd get there faster. Please hurry, he's hurt bad."

Twig sprinted to his horse and was gone in a flash. Galen Reid sauntered into the Irishman without a care in the world.

Within ten minutes, Twig slid to a halt beside the half-rebuilt barn. He spotted a man lying face down near a ladder—not moving. Twig gently grabbed the man's shoulder and rolled him over.

Wes Harms sneered up at him, his gun pointed at Twig's chest. Twig took a step back and raised his hands. Jeb Thompson hit him on the back of the head with a shovel.

****

Milo and Andy arrived back just as Newt and Jacob Brand raced toward Main Street, their arms waving wildly. Milo and Andy stopped, awaiting the speeding riders.

"Follow us," Newt shouted, barely slowing down.

Within fifty yards, the powerful hooves of Boots had brought Milo astride of the elder Brand. "What's the situation?"

"Trouble was brewing before," Newt yelled. "But, now Twig's missing."

"Where's the Mute?"

"Gone too." Newt filled Milo in on Rod Newby's status as a missing man.

"Shanks?"

"Still gone. So is Thompson,"

"Thompson," Milo muttered. "There's as good a place as any to start."

Their first stop was the office of Sturgis Rathbone. When Milo shouldered through the door, the judge was in the middle of hearing a case involving a disputed claim.

"Milo! Good to see you, but you'll have to wait…"

"Twig Randall is missing."

Sturgis stood. "You'll have to excuse me," he told the people at his desk. "Let's take a recess." His gaze turned to Milo. "What's this about?"

"Twig went missing this morning."

"That's the lot of them," Sturgis said. "All the local lawmen."

"Any idea where I might find Jeb Thompson?"

"He's nowhere near man enough to trifle with Twig."

"He's been after him since he donned the sheriff's badge." Milo snapped. "You got any better ideas?"

At that moment, Sam McLaren burst through the door, his breath coming in gulps. "Gunshots, out toward Reid's place."

Milo bolted for the door.

"You want I should ride with you?" Sam hollered after him.

"Sam's a dab hand with a gun," Sturgis added.

Milo yelled over his shoulder as he mounted his horse. "No, you stay put!"

As Milo passed the last building in town, a horse pulled abreast—Newt Brand had his rifle out and ready.

"Jacob's headed toward the shooting. I was on my way in to fetch you."

"Let's get," Milo shouted.

As they approached the notch surrounding Galen Reid's half-rebuilt house, Milo saw a wisp of dark smoke. By the time they saw Jacob behind the new barn, the smoke was thick. As they dismounted, the dirt in front of Newt's boot erupted. A loud crack followed instantly after. Milo grabbed Newt and pulled him to safety. Jacob waved them to his hiding spot.

"Someone's behind the rocks on the rise," Jacob said.

Another snap and a chunk of wood siding exploded above their heads.

"He'll pick us to pieces if we stay here," Milo said.

"If the fire don't get us first," Newt added.

Milo surveyed the land quickly. "We need to get over behind that mud wall beside the barn. It'll be out of the line of sight of anyone up high."

The three men stood to run and a third shot rang out. Milo's hat flew off and fell into an empty water trough nearby.

Jeb Thompson cursed when the big marshal didn't fall. He cocked his rifle and aimed again.

"Ease off the trigger, Jeb."

Thompson looked up, knowing the voice. "I thought I told you to run."

"I did," Rod Newby replied. "All the way here."

Thompson threw down the rifle. "Even if you kill me, Mute. Harms will hunt you down."

"I'll take my chances. Now, get up"

"You know I ain't going peaceful."

"I figured as much."

Thompson spun, his hand hitting his holster in a flash. The Mute beat him to it, his first shot hitting Thomson in the throat.

"That one's for Shanks," Newby said to the choking man.

Thompson looked at the sky, then back at the Mute. The blood in his throat stopping any final words.

Newby raised his weapon and shot Thompson through his meager heart. "And that one's for me."

In the lull, Milo raised his head for a peek. "Those two shots weren't a rifle."

The Brands laid still, waiting for another volley from above.

The next sound was a voice. "It's me, Marshal. Thompson's dead. All's clear!" Rod Newby stood on the berm, waving his hat.

As a thought came to him, Milo held out his arm to the Brands. "This is a trap. Thompson was a simple diversion." He pointed. "Twig's in the house. He's the cheese."

Newt nodded toward the smoke. "The fire's also to draw our attention."

A shot rang out from the house, slamming into the rock wall to Milo's left. The men dropped. Milo thought quickly. "Here's what we're going to do."

On the count of three, the men jumped to their feet, firing toward the window where the shot came from. Milo branched left and the Brands went right. As Newt and Jacob ran past the barn, Newt motioned. "Lay down some cover fire. I'll check on the smoke."

Seconds later, Newt's head popped back into view. "He lit a half-burnt hay pile afire. It ran its course."

Jacob grinned at his dad. "Just as you thought—a distraction."

More shots rang out, kicking up the soil near Milo's head. *I knew it was me he's after.*

When he neared a set of stables, Milo leapt behind a heavy wooden loading ramp. It immediately exploded, splinters flying everywhere.

Seeing Newt and Jacob disappear behind the cover of the partially re-built barn, Milo took a peek to assess the situation. The man in the window stood stock-still, arms outstretched, a black derby atop his head. A gun popped up and fired again, striking the post above him.

Think, Milo, think.

Jacob fired a shot from the barn, followed by another from Newby's position, both peppering the jamb of the house's front window. Milo chanced another glance and froze. The man in the window hadn't moved an inch—even under fire. The gun popped up and fired again. The man with the derby squirmed but didn't move.

Jacob and Newby returned fire, sending showers of wood in every direction.

Milo's thoughts cleared and he hollered, "Cease fire!"

A shot skipped off the ground in front of him. Milo slithered along to bottom of the corral toward the house. The wood erupted above where his head had been.

Exactly as he'd planned.

When he was out of the line of sight of the front window, Milo scuttled like a lizard to the rear of the house and eased through the back door. Wes Harms stood off to the side, his eyes toward the front yard, his back to Milo. Intermittently he'd swing his rifle up and fire, then bring it back down to cover the squirming man held in place by ropes in the front window—a black derby with a hawk feather in its band atop his head. The trussed man's body was barely as wide as the rope that bound him.

Twig!

Knowing that the next incoming bullet could mean the end of his friend's life, Milo watched Harms' every move, waiting for the right time to act.

Suddenly, Jacob Brand stepped into view in the yard, his rifle pointed directly at Twig Randall.

"No, Jacob!" Milo yelled.

Harms reacted like a cat—both men raised their guns simultaneously.

"Well," Harms sneered. "If it ain't my least-favorite cripple?"

"A touch of a surprise to see you, Wes. Seems to me, last I heard you were dead."

"I ain't dead, and I don't plan to be neither."

"Why'd you set this trap? You've already got the sheriff tied up. Who else were you looking for?"

"We figured Sam McLaren and a group of rag-tags might ride out." Harms sneered. "But mainly I wanted you."

"You were going to ambush the whole town?"

Harms nodded. "Anyone who doesn't recognize me as the new owner."

"Well," Milo said. "There's been a slight change of plans. First off, there is no we—Thompson's dead."

Harms jaw tightened.

"Secondly, since I'm here, you have to deal with me."

"And me," Andy Steele stepped into the room, his gun covering Harms.

Milo grinned. "And Andy."

"To hell with you both." Harms fired at the same time as Milo and Andy.

Milo clutched his side and dropped; his shirt immediately stained with blood.

Harms stumbled, then lunged behind a low counter. He fired another shot and shuffled toward the door. Andy belly-crawled behind a leather couch, his eyes darting back and forth between Milo and the last place he'd seen Harms. Taking a chance, he poked his head out and called to Milo.

A bullet ripped through the couch, sending stuffing and splinters everywhere. Andy moved again, chancing another glance.

Milo was gone.

Andy panicked. "Milo!"

When Harms raised his pistol, Milo acted, jumping over a table and landing atop the gunman. Harms got the shot off, but it flew wildly down the hall. Milo punched him, but Harms countered with a headbutt across the bridge of Milo's nose.

Seeing an opening, Harms raised his weapon. "See you in hell, Cripple."

Without thinking, Milo reached for his boot.

Andy heard a brief scuffle followed by a spluttering noise. His heart dropped. "Milo!"

"I'm right here," the big marshal replied. "It's safe."

Andy jumped to Milo's aid, stepping over the prone body of Wes Harms.

"I didn't hear…"

Milo pointed to Harms. The bone handle of a Bowie knife jutted from the soft underbelly of his chin, its blade settling somewhere inside the dead-man's brain.

"A knife?" Andy asked.

212

"Had to," Milo replied. "I dropped my dadgum Peacemaker when he shot me."

Andy gasped at the blood on Milo's shirt.

"It's a through and through," Milo groaned and went to his knees. "It'll bleed, but I'm fine. Help Twig."

Andy pulled his own knife and cut the restraints off Twig Randall.

When freed, Twig rushed to Milo. "Did he get you good?"

"Bleeding's almost stopped," Milo said. "But, dammit!"

"What?" Twig asked. "What's the matter?"

"That's a hole in my hat and a ruined shirt all in the span of one day."

The two men shared a chuckle—until they saw Andy Steele. He was standing over the lifeless form of Wes Harms, his face a mask of pain.

"He killed Clancy," Andy muttered. "And so many others. But, why?"

"Figured the world owed him something," Twig said.

"The world owes us nothing." Andy's eyes filled with tears. "You make your own way."

Without warning, he kicked Harms' body, then recoiled at his own outburst.

Milo put his hand on Andy's shoulder. "That's enough. He's paid the price."

"There's no price high enough for what he's done," Andy said. "You can't assess a value on what he tore asunder."

"Wisdom like that's learned living life," Twig sighed. "They don't teach lessons like that in college."

Milo took his hand off Andy's shoulder and sighed. When the other men looked, he pointed to the big, red handprint on the young man's shirt. "Looks like Andy learned a way for me to buy him some new clothes."

Twig grew serious. "That's the second time you've saved my bacon, Milo. I'm much obliged."

"Well, now that we've killed off all the bad fellas in town, maybe you can keep a lid on things."

"They ain't all been corralled," Twig reminded him. "Even if he can't shoot a gun—Galen Reid's the most dangerous of the lot."

Twig led the men to the rise, where they found Rod Newby eating an apple from Reid's orchard. The smile on the Mute's face grew with each friend that came into view. "Nice to see you all. I heard a lot of shooting going on down there."

"And we heard quite a bit from up here." Milo glanced at Jeb Thompson's body, then back to the Mute. "Thanks for covering the high ground."

"Jeb always was more bluster than brains." Newby's eyes widened and he pointed at the red stain on the big marshal's shirt. "You're hit, Milo."

"Harms rushed his shot. Barely clipped my side. The bleedings already stopped."

"Is Wes dead?" Newby asked.

"Thanks to Milo and Andy" Twig replied.

Newby's eyes shifted to the young man standing next to Milo. He tossed his apple aside, wiped his hands on his britches, and extended his right hand. "I owe you an apology, Mister Steele. I don't have the words to say how sorry I am for what I put you through."

Andy accepted the Newby's hand and the two men shook.

"When I met you the first time at the campfire you seemed the kind of man I could be friends with," Andy said. "I'm willing to extend a second chance."

"Fair enough. As a gesture of friendship, I'll help you find your cousin."

Andy's eyes dropped. "He's dead. Wes Harms saw to that."

Newby shook his head. "That's news I'm very sorry to hear. We're all better off Wes is dead. He killed Shanks."

Twig's eyes widened. "Shanks is dead? Jeb told me…"

"Yeah, well, Wes and Jeb threatened me with a bullet, as well."

"We thought you lit out," Twig said. "Why'd you stay?"

"I knew Jeb was up to something when he told me to run away for good." He grinned. "Fortunately, he's not my boss, so I didn't follow his orders."

"That there's some clever thinking," Milo grinned. "I'm glad you stuck around, Rod. You saved our hide."

"Just doing my job, Marshal. The way Alf would've wanted me to."

CHAPTER THIRTY-TWO

Furious with the failed ambush, less-so about the demise of its perpetrators, Galen Reid stalked into McLaren's Dry Goods, summoning the proprietor out of reach of prying ears. "You heard of those fools' attempt on the wanna-be sheriff's life?"

"Yep," Sam shrugged.

"Well, what's your take on the matter."

Sam thought for a moment. *Play him false, dig as much as you can from his pea-brain.* "Wasn't a very well thought out plan."

Reid keyed on McLaren's moderation, mistaking it for complicity. His voice dropped. "We've got to get rid of Sturgis and all the outsiders, Sam. They're putting a crimp in Loess' growth."

"How do you figure that?"

Reid's eyes narrowed. "I thought you were on my side, Sam. But now I can see you're just non-committal. Well, they've got to go, whether you help or not." Reid stomped across the floor and yanked the door open. "I'll just take care of things myself."

Before the noise of the slamming door abated, Sam McLaren disappeared out the back of his store, appearing almost instantly in the Sheriff's office. Not giving Twig or Milo a chance to speak, Sam blurted. "You're in danger, Twig."

"Seems like I always am."

McLaren shook his head. "This time it's Reid himself. He says both you and Sturgis have to go and he's sold himself that you're an enemy of Loess. He's got enough money to hire some tough men. They might come from a couple of angles."

"Thanks, Sam. I'll inform Sturgis." Twig thrust his shoulders back. "It's about time we resolve this."

When Sam was gone, Twig turned to Milo. "The fat's in the fire now."

Milo snatched up pencil and paper and hastily scratched out a note. "I have an idea, Twig. Find the Mute, then you two stay out of sight and follow these instructions." He nodded and disappeared across the street.

Within minutes, Milo knocked on a shabby office door and a reedy voice summoned him inside. Galen Reid sat behind his desk, tallying figures on a yellowed piece of parchment. "Ah, Marshal, I'm glad you're in town. I have some criminal information on Judge Rathbone that might interest you— murder even."

Milo knew his hunch was correct. *He doesn't know that I know.* "That's what I'm down here investigating, Mister Reid. State your case."

Reid proceeded to tell Milo the false version of the Clancy Walker story. Pausing for dramatic emphasis when appropriate.

When he'd finished, Milo sat back. "I'm afraid I'm going to have to haul the codger in."

"Hang him from that confounded Widowmaker he loves so much," Reid crowed with a self-satisfied grin.

"We could, except there's no branches left on it."

Reid's brow furrowed.

"The overzealous fool hung so many men he plum wore the branch out." Milo leaned in. "Why don't we get him good? I'll ask Sam McLaren to organize a town meeting at sunset tonight. You can tell everyone what happened and they'll run Sturgis out of town on a rail. Once he hits the city limits, I'll arrest him." Milo sat back and crossed his arms in satisfaction.

Reid's eyes widened. "You'd help me in such a manner?"

"Yes, of course. After all, my job is to root out evil. We certainly don't need scoundrels like that in Kansas."

Reid's piggy smile sealed the deal.

That evening, Milo stepped onto the raised boardwalk in front of the courthouse to find the entire citizenry of Loess gathered in the street. He drew his hog-leg and fired a shot toward the heavens, effectively calling the town meeting to order.

"Ladies and gentlemen, I present you the esteemed owner of Loess, Galen Reid."

Reid gave a half-bow and cleared his throat. "I am here tonight to speak of a heinous matter, one that strikes to the very core of our little town. It pains me to say it, but Judge Sturgis Rathbone is a murderer."

The crowd gave a collective gasp.

"I know, I know," Reid went on. "Shocking as it may seem, Judge Rathbone and our late Sheriff, Alf Lemure, shot a young man by the name of Clancy Walker in front of me and my ward, the late Wesley Harms." Reid paused for effect, wiping his eyes with a hanky. "It has taken me this long to find my voice, but found it I have. Judge Sturgis Rathbone is a murderer."

"String him up!" one man yelled.

Galen Reid took a confident step back, pleased to have sentiment on his side.

Milo stepped to the side of the stage and led Sturgis to the forefront. Milo then addressed the townsfolk. "As a Deputy Marshal from the Great State of Kansas, it is my duty to place Judge Rathbone under arrest for murder."

"No arrest," another man yelled. "String him up!"

Milo went silent as they worked themselves into a frenzy. He drew out his weapon and fired a second shot to the stars. The crowd quieted.

"All right, I've heard what you want, we'll string him up instead."

The mob roared.

"But, first..."

They fell silent.

"I need to give any witnesses a chance to speak. Does anyone have anything to add?"

A handsome man, dressed in black stepped forward. "I do."

"State your name and spill the beans," Milo said.

"My name is Andy Steele. I was Clancy Walker's cousin."

Galen Reid's face flushed at the unexpected witness, but his heart nearly stopped when Twig Randall and Rod Newby stepped into view—two men he thought dead.

Andy went on. "I was there when Wes Harms died. He told the entire tale of Clancy's murder to Marshal Thorne and myself."

Heads turned, searching each other for how to react next. When no one set the tone, all eyes went back to Andy.

"Go on," Milo prompted.

"This is the story Wes Harms related: He set fire to Galen Reid's house in an effort to burn him to death."

Reid tried to shout an objection, but his words were drowned out by a rebuke from the frenzied mob.

"Wes Harms killed Alf Lemure with a hammer blow to the side of his head, while you all fought the fire at Galen Reid's house."

A rumbling spread amongst the townspeople, requiring a third shot by Milo. "Let him speak!"

"During the fire at Reid's house, Marshal Thorne cornered Harms next to Alf's body, but Harms got the drop on him with Alf's gun. Not satisfied with taking the Marshal's life quick-like, Harms taunted his quarry. From the hay loft directly above them, I heard Harms brag to the Marshal about killing Clancy over gambling losses and framing Sheriff Lemure and Judge Rathbone. It was Galen Reid who came up with the fraudulent story and he's been using it to blackmail them ever since."

"This is an outrage," Reid yelled. "Wes would never act as such!"

"Harms was a brute!" a woman yelled.

"Ran roughshod over Loess," another man added.

Twig cut across them. "Quiet! Let the witness finish."

Out of respect to the new town Sheriff, the crowd silenced.

Andy took a deep breath. "Before Harms could kill Marshal Thorne, I accidentally knocked both of them down when the loft caught fire. In the confusion, Harms escaped."

"String the bumbling fool up!" someone yelled. "He freed a murderer!"

"Wait!" Milo bellowed. "Hear him out!"

Andy went on. "After the fire, Harms acted in cahoots with Jeb Thompson to murder Shanks Morris."

A collective gasp went up. "Not Shanks!"

"How do you know this?" Reid yelled. "It rings false!"

"I can vouch for every word as true," Rod Newby chimed in. "Harms and Thompson tried to run me off. They admitted to killing Shanks. They kidnapped Twig, and tried to kill me."

"But we're here," Twig added. "Must be quite the shock for you, Galen?"

The crowd grumbled, processing the information.

"I say we string Reid up for the whole mess!" someone yelled.

They began to chant. "String up Reid!"

Judge Rathbone stepped forward. "Harms murdered Clancy Walker. Reid was just an accessory. I've got no call to hang him."

"That's right!" Reid wailed. "And I had no knowledge Wes was alive after the fire. I certainly had nothing to do with the kidnapping of the sheriff."

"That's a lie!" someone yelled.

"Who said that?" Reid hissed. "Who dares call me a liar?"

"I do." Spike Duggan stepped to the forefront. "I saw Harms and Thompson enter a room at the Broken Shoe with you a week after the fire."

The chant started anew. "String up Reid!"

"Go on home and leave me be," Reid yelled, his face registering terror.

"Stick around Loess and you're a dead man," someone yelled.

Reid's face contorted in rage. "You ungrateful bunch of heathens. After all I've done…"

"Once again," Sturgis called to the crowd. "Reid is a simple accessory. It was Harms and Thompson who killed Shanks Morris. I can't charge him."

Reid spat and stomped for the stairs, fleeing toward safety—until Milo grabbed his arm. "I'd be careful around here if I were you."

"I've no want to stay here," Reid hissed. "But I'm heavily invested."

As the man ranted, Milo realized his words were empty. *He's insolvent.* "You don't have two nickels to rub together, do you, Reid?"

Reid's resolve broke. "Wes stole the last money in my mother's estate." He glared at the big marshal; his words bitter. "The last money I had in the world. My inheritance has been keeping me afloat, but it's gone."

The crowd erupted in laughter at Reid's financial demise.

Milo looked upon the man with something akin to pity. From nowhere, he recalled Mort Grange's telegram. *What good does it do me to be the richest man in Vermont when I live here?*

"I'll give you three-thousand dollars cash for everything you own," Milo offered. "Under one condition."

Reid's eyes widened. "What's that?"

"You get on a horse and ride out, never to return to these parts."

"You'll see me safely to Kansas City?"

"I don't want you there either," Milo replied.

"I can catch a train back to Boston from there."

"We leave first thing in the morning."

The crowd erupted in cheers, and the evening sky filled with tossed hats and celebratory gunfire. As Galen Reid disappeared into the Irishman, the Randalls and Brands rushed to Milo.

"We heard everything," May blurted. "Congratulations, Milo!"

Milo turned to Twig. "Loess still needs a sheriff, you interested? It comes with property, but we'll have to rebuild the house."

May and Twig looked at each other, their eyes curious.

"The Reid place." Milo went on. "Next to the river, best water rights in Kansas, easy walking distance to Langer's Hole."

Milo looked at Newt and then back to Twig. "There's plenty of land for two homes."

May glanced from Maggie to Sara and back to Maggie. Maggie gave an imperceptible nod.

"Is there enough for three homes?" May asked.

Milo smiled. "Plenty. Plus, it crossed my mind that this town could use a school and a diner."

May Randall didn't hesitate. "This here's where we'll call home—the lot of us."

Smiling, Twig turned to Newt and Jacob. "The new sheriff'll be needing some help here. You two interested?"

Newt and Jacob nodded in unison.

Twig rounded on his friend—now boss: "You've got yourself a sheriff."

Those hats that hadn't been tossed finally flew into the darkness.

Milo addressed the still gathered townsfolk. "As you heard, Galen Reid is no more. Loess is mine, from the birds in the trees down to the dust on the street."

The crowd applauded its approval.

"Whatever property you live on is now yours to keep. Stake your claim with the newly appointed Mayor, Sam McLaren."

The crowd roared, but there wasn't a hat left to be thrown.

"Just do me one favor," Milo laughed. "Leave some fish in Langer's Hole for when I come to visit."

When the townsfolk had finally dispersed, Milo's lone hand was raw for shaking that of every man, woman, and child in town. Twig tugged at his sleeve and motioned him to a quiet place on the sidewalk.

"I don't know what to say," Twig muttered. "But, thank you."

"That's plenty."

Without speaking, Twig handed Milo a sealed envelope marked: *For Silas Petit.* Twig turned to leave.

"I was being selfish before."

"When?"

"Back when I wanted you to come home to Kansas City." Milo gazed up at the stars. "But you deserve happiness, and I think you and yours will fit right in here. You, May, the Brands—all of you."

Twig nodded, unable to speak.

"And that makes *me* happy."

"I understand that now." Twig looked up at his big friend and shook his head. "You never cease to amaze me, Milo. You'd give away your last nickel, if you ever got that short in your pocket."

"If it'd make someone happy," Milo grinned, "I surely would."

Twig gave a nod and a smile in response.

"But," Milo chuckled, "since I'm paying your salary now—"

Twig's eyebrows shot up at the notion.

"—you'd better thank your stars that I've got a big stack of nickels."

CHAPTER THIRTY-THREE

Milo, Andy, and Galen Reid left before first light, setting a brisk pace north. As it wasn't a pleasure trip, all eyes were forward and no one spoke. On the outskirts of town, a fourth set of hoofbeats joined the travel party when Rod Newby fell into pace.

"Headed out, Mute?" Milo asked.

Newby shrugged. "I was beholden to Alf. Now that he's dead, I'm free to roam."

"Where are you headed," Milo asked.

"Where are you going?"

"You know where we're going."

"I kinda want to give the big city life a try. It's a natural move."

"How's that?"

"I kind of like this talking stuff. More folks, equals more conversation."

Milo chuckled. "Now you've started, we've got no means to shut you up."

****

When darkness made travel unsafe, Milo called a halt and camp was set up. They made a small fire, ate a sparse dinner and laid out under the stars to catch some winks. Reid slept away from the group, claiming the other men's snores would keep him awake. Newby waited until the fat man himself started snoring, then placed his bedroll close so he could keep an eye on the scoundrel.

Milo threw dirt on the fire and was nearly asleep when Andy spoke. "It doesn't upset me a bit that the Harms fellow is dead. He got his just deserts for killing Clancy over a few lousy dollars. Losing my cousin is a blow to the core of me."

"No one's going to hold you accountable for hating the man who killed your kin," Milo replied. "Just make sure that hate doesn't kill part of you, as well."

"How so?"

231

"Plenty of folks transfer hate of one person, or one personal failing, into a hatred for everyone and everything. They're still breathing, and their eyes still see, but their hearts become black as a bottomless cave."

Andy went silent for a moment. "What drives you to be a lawman, Marshal?"

Noting the depth of the question and the emotion behind it, Milo was quickly wide-awake. "A sense of satisfaction knowing I'm helping folks."

"Even folks like Reid over there?"

"Even Reid."

"But he fought you every step of the way, even when you were trying to help him."

Milo took his time with his next words. "He was hurting inside—just lost his last remaining relative. Folks do funny things when they're hurt." As soon as it left his mouth, Milo knew the second sentence could apply in myriad ways.

"Yet, at the fire, you risked your neck to save him. For the life of me, I can't reconcile such."

"I'd have saved Harms himself if the situation called for it."

Andy rolled onto his elbow. "Harms? Why on earth…"

"The badge on my chest and what it stands for."

Andy rolled onto his back, starring into the inky depths. "I don't get it."

"If I pinned on my star every morning, wishin' and hopin' for praise or glory, I'd have quit a long time ago," Milo said. "That type of thing doesn't hold sway with me. It all comes down to how I feel inside when I do what's right."

"The internal satisfaction outweighs the external reward."

"Spoken like a true college man," Milo chuckled. It was his turn to ask the deep question. "Why did you run back in the barn to save Alf Lemure's carcass after he hung you by mistake?"

"No matter what he'd done, I couldn't see letting the man burn when I could do something about it."

"Welcome to the light, Mister Steele."

****

When they reached Kansas City, Milo procured the necessary cash from the First Bank of Kansas and met Galen Reid at the train station.

"Here's your money, Reid."

"There's less than three-thousand dollars here. We agreed to—"

"I paid for your ticket to Boston out of your money. And for our lunch."

Reid put the cash in his pocket and snarled. "The joke's on you, you big fool. That lands only worth two-thousand, tops."

It was Milo's turn to laugh. "Actually, the jokes on you, Reid. I'd have paid six if you'd have asked."

Galen Reid's ears reddened. He picked up what little luggage he had and started onto the train.

"Oh, by the way," Milo said with a smirk. "I sent a telegram to an old friend of mine. He's the Chief Detective from the Boston Police Department. I told him *all* about you. He said he'd be *happy* to keep an eye out for you around town."

Reid's face dropped.

Milo gave the fat man a big smile. "Have a nice ride home."

Chuckling all the way, the three lawmen made a straight line for the Armory, and for Silas Petit. Bad news does not sit well on a man's shoulders.

Milo showed the two men into his own office. "Let me talk to Silas first," he said. "I've got something for him, then

I'll bring him in to see you." Milo padded his pockets with a blank look on his face. "Dang, it's in my saddle bag. Sit tight, I'll go fetch it."

Milo disappeared out the door. Less than ten minutes later, he reappeared to find Silas hastily looking through a stack of forms on a hallway desk.

"Welcome back," Silas said. "Meet me inside. Once I find the right paperwork, I've got a job for you."

Milo went into the boss's office and nearly fainted. Seated in a chair in front of Silas Petit's desk was Andy Steele—with a shiny Marshal's badge pinned to his chest.

Andy grinned at the look on Milo's face. "You should have seen this coming."

"Pleasant surprise indeed," Milo grinned back.

At that moment, Silas shuffled inside with the evasive form held high. "Milo, meet our newest Deputy Marshal, Andy Steele."

"We've met," the two men said in unison.

"That makes this easy," Silas replied as he handed Andy the form. "There's a pen on yonder desk. Fill this out, as best you can."

When Andy was gone, Milo squared on Silas. "Any idea who that man is?"

"He said you two were acquainted. He's a sharp fella."

"He's the man who Alf hung in error down in Loess."

"The Hampton lookalike?"

"One and the same."

Silas chuckled. "He came in and inquired about the position. He's got serious qualifications, Milo. As much, or more, as you did when you started. Sharp as a tack."

"Make no mistake, Boss, he has my approval."

"Good to hear," Silas said. "Since you'll be the one training him."

"That's a lot of responsibility. You sure you trust me that much?"

"Oh, yes, I trust you plenty."

"I'll do you proud." Milo waited a split second, knowing what was to come.

After a pause, Silas asked the question he'd never wanted to. "Did you get the sheriff situation squared away down there?"

Milo's eyes fell. "Yes, sir."

Silas read his reaction. "Twig take the job?"

"Yes, sir."

Silas fell back into his chair, as if the weight of the world had dropped on his shoulders. "Damn, I'm gonna miss the miserable cuss."

A furry puppy waddled through the door and stopped at Milo's feet. He scooped him up and began to rub his ears. "Good news is, Twig's only a day's ride away."

"How's that supposed to salve things?"

"You can visit him any time you please. Maybe you and Amy can vacation down that way."

"Where'd you get a cockamamie notion like that? Did he hire you to entice folks to Loess?"

"No," Milo chuckled. "I bought the town,"

Silas nearly fell over backward. "You bought Loess?"

"Lock, stock, and barrel."

Silas cottoned on quickly and began to chuckle. "Twig's your employee now, huh?"

"I never wanted this to come to pass," Milo grinned. "But, I've said all along that I want my friends to be happy. So, I figured I'd help bring it to fruition."

"You've come a long way from *change ain't fair*."

"There's a freedom in knowing it isn't," Milo sighed. "It helps a man live for the *now* instead of for the *someday*."

237

"That there's a lesson no amount of money can purchase."

Silas smiled and held out his hands. Milo reluctantly relinquished the dog.

"Who's this?"

"His name's Pete. His sister's a Randall, lives with the new sheriff and his wife."

Silas smiled and rubbed under Pete's chin. "Needless to say, our loss is their gain. This job grinds forward no matter who's behind the badge."

"Twig asked me to give you this." Milo handed Silas the envelope.

Silas,

No doubt Milo has told you I've accepted the Loess Sheriff   job. May and I will be back in town soon to tie up loose   ends. You and yours are always welcome here. My only wish   moving forward is to be half the leader for my men that you   were to me. For that, I thank you.

Your friend, Twig

"How is he?" Silas asked.

"Like a pig in a garbage dump. Gonna need a new face, because he's plumb smiled the old one off."

"Losing him's gonna leave holes," Silas sighed. "Gonna be tough to replace."

"Andy's a good start," Milo replied. "He handled himself well in the shootout with Wes Harms." Milo rubbed his side. "Better even than I did."

"Still, it'll take him some time to get trained up and seasoned."

"Well, this ought to brighten your spirits some. Rod Newby rode north with me, looking for a change."

"The Mute? I'd hire him in a hot second."

"Good. He's waiting for you in my office."

Silas laughed. "I said it the first time I met you, Milo, and I'll say it again—we'll all end up working for you someday."

THE END

Acknowledgments

A HUGE thank you goes out to the members of the Saugus Cafe Writing Group. This book would not have been possible without the input and wisdom of Toni Floyd, Bill Lyons, Tom Tucker and Gordon Lazarus.

Another HUGE thank you goes out to my wife, Lynn for her assistance in reading and editing this manuscript—and for generally keeping me in line. I love you!

As always, this is for my family: Lynn and Elizabeth. You are my inspiration!

Last, and certainly not least, THANK YOU to those precious friends who have read and commented on my previous books. I'm so glad you enjoy them!

Stay tuned for the soon to be published FINAL adventure of:

Marshal Milo Thorne, Frontier Philosopher

Grave Measures

In case you missed them, the first four books of the series;

The Crooked Trail,

Bloodshot Sunset,

Halo or Horns,

And Culpepper Gulch,

are all available through Amazon.

Made in the USA
Columbia, SC
12 February 2023

11718992R00150